Hope and Other Dangerous Pursuits

Hope
& Other
Dangerous
Pursuits

Laila Lalami

ALGONQUIN BOOKS
OF CHAPEL HILL
2005

Published by
ALGONQUIN BOOKS OF CHAPEL HILL
Post Office Box 2225
Chapel Hill, North Carolina 27515-2225

a division of
Workman Publishing
708 Broadway
New York, New York 10003

Some of the stories in this collection appeared in somewhat different form
in the following magazines: "The Trip" in *First Intensity*; "Better Luck
Tomorrow" in *The Baltimore Review*.

The version of the enchanted rug story used in "The Storyteller" is taken
from *Contes et Légendes du Maroc*, Editions Fernand-Nathan, 1955.

This is a work of fiction. While, as in all fiction, the literary perceptions and
insights are based on experience, all names, characters, places, and incidents
are either products of the author's imagination or are used fictitiously. No
reference to any real person is intended or should be inferred.

Library of Congress Cataloging-in-Publication Data
Lalami, Laila, 1968–
    Hope and other dangerous pursuits / Laila Lalami.—1st ed.
      p. cm.
    ISBN-13: 978-1-56512-493-6
    ISBN-10: 1-56512-493-6
    1. Moroccans—Spain—Fiction.   2. Immigrants—Fiction.
  3. Lifeboats—Fiction.   4. Morocco—Fiction.   5. Spain—Fiction.
  I. Title.
  PS3612.A543H68 2005
  813'.6—dc22   2005047821

10 9 8 7 6 5 4 3 2 1
First Edition

For Alexander

CONTENTS

Hope and Other Dangerous Pursuits

The Trip

FOURTEEN KILOMETERS. Murad has pondered that number hundreds of times in the last year, trying to decide whether the risk was worth it. Some days he told himself that the distance was nothing, a brief inconvenience, that the crossing would take as little as thirty minutes if the weather was good. He spent hours thinking about what he would do once he was on the other side, imagining the job, the car, the house. Other days he could think only about the coast guards, the ice-cold water, the money he'd have to borrow, and he wondered how fourteen kilometers could separate not just two countries but two universes.

Tonight the sea appears calm, with only a slight wind

now and then. The captain has ordered all the lights turned off, but with the moon up and the sky clear, Murad can still see around him. The six-meter Zodiac inflatable is meant to accommodate eight people. Thirty huddle in it now, men, women, and children, all with the anxious look of those whose destinies are in the hands of others—the captain, the coast guards, God.

Murad has three layers on: undershirt, turtleneck, and jacket; below, a pair of thermal underwear, jeans, and sneakers. With only three hours' notice, he didn't have time to get waterproof pants. He touches a button on his watch, a Rolex knockoff he bought from a street vendor in Tangier, and the display lights up: 3:15 A.M. He scratches at the residue the metal bracelet leaves on his wrist, then pulls his sleeve down to cover the timepiece. Looking around him, he can't help but wonder how much Captain Rahal and his gang stand to make. If the other passengers paid as much as Murad did, the take is almost 600,000 dirhams, enough for an apartment or a small house in a Moroccan beach town like Asilah or Cabo Negro.

He looks at the Spanish coastline, closer with every breath. The waves are inky black, except for hints of foam here and there, glistening white under the moon, like tombstones in a dark cemetery. Murad can make out the town where they're headed. Tarifa. The mainland point of the Moorish invasion in 711. Murad used to regale tourists with anecdotes about how Tariq Ibn Ziyad had led a powerful Moor army across the Straits and, upon landing in Gibraltar, ordered all the boats burned. He'd told his soldiers that they could march forth and defeat the enemy or turn back and die a coward's death. The men had followed their general, toppled the Visigoths, and established an empire that ruled over Spain for more than seven hundred years. Little did they know that we'd be back, Murad thinks. Only instead of a fleet, here we are in an inflatable boat—not just Moors, but a motley mix of people from the ex-colonies, without guns or armor, without a charismatic leader.

It's worth it, though, Murad tells himself. Some time on this flimsy boat and then a job. It will be hard at first. He'll work in the fields like everyone else, but he'll look for something better. He isn't like the others—he has a plan. He doesn't want to break his back for the *spagnol,* spend the rest of his life picking their oranges and tomatoes. He'll find a real job, where he can use his training. He has a degree in English and, in addition, he speaks Spanish fluently, unlike some of the harraga.

His leg goes numb. He moves his ankle around. To his

left, the girl (he thinks her name is Faten) shifts slightly, so that her thigh no longer presses against his. She looks eighteen, nineteen maybe. "My leg was asleep," he whispers. Faten nods to acknowledge him but doesn't look at him. She pulls her black cardigan tight around her chest and stares down at her shoes. He doesn't understand why she's wearing a hijab scarf on her hair for a trip like this. Does she imagine she can walk down the street in Tarifa in a headscarf without attracting attention? She'll get caught, he thinks.

Back on the beach, while they all were waiting for Rahal to get ready, Faten sat alone, away from everyone else, as though she were sulking. She was the last one to climb into the boat, and Murad had to move to make room for her. He couldn't understand her reluctance. It didn't seem possible to him that she would have paid so much money and not been eager to leave when the moment came.

Across from Murad is Aziz. He's tall and lanky and he sits hunched over to fit in the narrow space allotted to him. This is his second attempt at crossing the Strait of Gibraltar. He told Murad that he'd haggled with Rahal over the price of the trip, argued that, as a repeat customer, he should get a deal. Murad tried to bargain, too, but in the end he still had to borrow almost 20,000 dirhams from one of his uncles, and the loan is on his mind again. He'll pay his uncle back as soon as he can get a job.

Aziz asks for a sip of water. Murad hands over his bottle of Sidi Harazem and watches him take a swig. When he gets the bottle back, he offers the last bit to Faten, but she shakes her head. Murad was told he should keep his body hydrated, so he's been drinking water all day. He feels a sudden urge to urinate and leans forward to contain it.

Next to Aziz is a middle-aged man with greasy hair and a large scar across his cheek, like Al Pacino in *Scarface*. He wears jeans and a short-sleeved shirt. Murad heard him tell someone that he was a tennis instructor. His arms are muscular, his biceps bulging, but the energy he exudes is rough, like that of a man used to trouble with the law. Murad notices that Scarface has been staring at the little girl sitting next to him. She seems to be about ten years old, but the expression on her face is that of an older child. Her eyes, shiny under the moonlight, take up most of her face. Scarface asks her name. "Mouna," she says. He reaches into his pocket and offers her chewing gum, but the girl quickly shakes her head.

Her mother, Halima, asked Murad the time before they got on the boat, as though she had a schedule to keep. She gives Scarface a dark, forbidding look, wraps one arm around her daughter and the other around her two boys, seated to her right. Halima's gaze is direct, not shifty like Faten's. She has an aura of quiet determination about her, and it stirs feelings of respect in Murad, even though he thinks her irresponsible, or at the very least foolish, for risking her children's lives on a trip like this.

On Aziz's right is a slender African woman, her corn-rows tied in a loose ponytail. While they were waiting on the beach to depart, she peeled an orange and offered Murad half. She said she was Guinean. She cradles her body with her arms and rocks gently back and forth. Rahal barks at her to stop. She looks up, tries to stay immobile, and then throws up on Faten's boots. Faten cries out at the sight of her sullied shoes.

"Shut up," Rahal snaps.

The Guinean woman whispers an apology in French. Faten waves her hand, says that it's okay, says she understands. Soon the little boat reeks of vomit. Murad tucks his nose inside his turtleneck. It smells of soap and mint and it keeps out the stench, but within minutes the putrid smell penetrates the shield anyway. Now Halima sits up and exhales loudly, her children still huddling next to her. Rahal glares at her, tells her to hunch down to keep the boat balanced.

"Leave her alone," Murad says.

Halima turns to him and smiles for the first time. He wonders what her plans are, whether she's meeting a husband or a brother there or if she'll end up cleaning houses or working in the fields. He thinks about some of the illegals who, instead of going on a boat, try to sneak in on vegetable trucks headed from Morocco to Spain. Last year the Guardia Civil intercepted a tomato truck in Algeciras and found the bodies of three illegals, dead from asphyxiation, lying on the crates. At least on a boat there is no chance of that happening. He tries to think of something else, something to chase away the memory of the picture he saw in the paper.

The outboard motor idles. In the sudden silence, everyone turns to look at Rahal, collectively holding their breath. "Shit," he says between his teeth. He pulls the starter cable a few times, but nothing happens.

"What's wrong?" Faten asks, her voice laden with anxiety.

Rahal doesn't answer.

"Try again," Halima says.

Rahal yanks at the cable.

"This trip is cursed," Faten whispers. Everyone hears her.

Rahal bangs the motor with his hand. Faten recites a verse from the second sura of the Qur'an: " 'God, there is no God but Him, the Alive, the Eternal. Neither slumber nor sleep overtaketh Him—' "

"Quiet," Scarface yells. "We need some quiet to think." Looking at the captain, he asks, "Is it the spark plug?"

"I don't know. I don't think so," says Rahal.

Faten continues to pray, this time more quietly, her lips moving fast. " 'Unto Him belongeth all that is in the heavens and the earth . . .' "

Rahal yanks at the cable again.

Aziz calls out, "Wait, let me see." He gets on all fours, over the vomit, and moves slowly to keep the boat stable.

Faten starts crying, a long and drawn-out whine. All eyes are on her. Her hysteria is contagious, and Murad can hear someone sniffling at the other end of the boat.

"What are you crying for?" Scarface asks, leaning forward to look at her face.

"I'm afraid," she whimpers.

"Baraka!" he orders.

"Leave her be," Halima says, still holding her children close.

"Why did she come if she can't handle it?" he yells, pointing at Faten.

Murad pulls his shirt down from his face. "Who the hell do you think you are?" He's the first to be surprised by his anger. He is tense and ready for an argument.

"And who are you?" Scarface says. "Her protector?"

A cargo ship blows its horn, startling everyone. It glides in the distance, lights blinking.

"Stop it," Rahal yells. "Someone will hear us!"

Aziz examines the motor, pulls at the hose that connects it to the tank. "There's a gap here," he tells Rahal, and he points to the connector. "Do you have some tape?" Rahal opens his supplies box and takes out a roll of duct tape. Aziz quickly wraps some around the hose. The captain pulls the cable once, twice. Finally the motor wheezes painfully and the boat starts moving.

"Praise be to God," Faten says, ignoring Scarface's glares.

The crying stops and a grim peace falls on the boat.

TARIFA IS ABOUT 250 meters away now. It'll only take another few minutes. The Guinean woman throws a piece of paper overboard. Murad figures it's her ID. She'll probably pretend she's from Sierra Leone so she can get political asylum. He shakes his head. No such luck for him.

The water is still calm, but Murad knows better than to trust the Mediterranean. He's known the sea all his life and he knows how hard it can pull. Once, when he was ten years old, he went mussel picking with his father at the beach in Al Hoceima. As they were working away, Murad saw a dark, beautiful bed of mussels hanging from their beards inside a hollow rock. He lowered himself in and was busy pulling at them when a wave filled the grotto and flushed him out. His father grabbed Murad, still holding the bucket, out of the water. Later, Murad's father would tell his friends at the café an adorned version of this story, which would be added to his repertoire of family tales that he narrated on demand.

"Everyone out of the boat now!" Rahal shouts. "You have to swim the rest of the way."

Aziz immediately rolls out into the water and starts swimming.

Like the other passengers, Murad looks on, stunned. They expected to be taken all the way to the shore, where they could easily disperse and then hide. The idea of having to swim the rest of the way is intolerable, especially for those who are not natives of Tangier and accustomed to its waters.

Halima raises a hand at Rahal. "You thief! We paid you to take us to the coast."

Rahal says, "You want to get us all arrested a harraga? Get out of the boat if you want to get there. It's not that far. I'm turning back."

Someone makes an abrupt movement to reason with Rahal, to force him to go all the way to the shore, but the Zodiac loses balance and then it's too late. Murad is in the water now. His clothes are instantly wet, and the shock of the cold water all over his body makes his heart go still for a moment. He bobs, gasps for air, realizes that there's nothing left to do but swim. So he wills his limbs, heavy with the weight of his clothes, to move.

Around him, people are slowly scattering, led by the crosscurrents. Rahal struggles to right his boat and someone, Murad can't quite tell who, is hanging on to the side. He hears howls and screams, sees a few people swimming in earnest. Aziz, who was first to get out of the boat, is already far ahead of the others, going west. Murad starts swimming toward the coast, afraid he might be pulled away by the water. From behind, he hears someone call out. He turns and holds his hand out to Faten. She grabs it and the next second she is holding both his shoulders. He tries to pull away, but her grip tightens.

"Use one hand to move," he yells.

Her eyes open wider but her hands do not move. He forces one of her hands off him and manages to make a few strokes. Her body is heavy against his. Each time they bob in the water, she holds on tighter. There is water in his ears now and her cries are not as loud. He tries to loosen her grip but she won't let go. He yells out. Still she holds on. The next time they bob, water enters his nose and it makes him cough. They'll never make it if she doesn't loosen her grip and help him. He pushes her away. Free at last, he moves quickly out of her reach. "Beat the water with your arms," he yells. She thrashes wildly. "Slower," he tells her, but he can see that it is hopeless, she can't swim. A sob forms in his throat. If only he had a stick or a buoy that he could hand her so that he could pull her without risking that they both drown. He's already drifting away from her, but he keeps calling out, telling her to calm down and start swimming. His fingers and toes have gone numb, and he has to start swimming or he'll freeze to death. He faces the coast. He closes his eyes, but the image of Faten is waiting for him behind the lids. Eyes open again, he tries to focus on the motion of his limbs.

There is a strange quietness in the air. He swims until he feels the sand against his feet. He tries to control his breathing, the beating of his heart in his ears. He lies on the beach, the water licking his shoes. The sun is rising, painting the sand and the buildings far ahead a golden shade of orange. With a sigh, Murad relieves his bladder. The sand around him warms up but cools again in seconds. He rests there for a little while, then pushes himself to his knees.

He stands, legs shaking. He turns around and scans the dark waters, looking for Faten. He can see a few forms swimming, struggling, but it's hard to tell who is who. Aziz is nowhere to be seen, but the Guinean woman is getting out of the water a few meters away.

In the distance, a dog barks.

Murad knows he doesn't have much time before the Guardia Civil come after them. He takes a few steps and drops to his knees on the sand, which feels warmer than the water. With a trembling hand, he opens a side pocket of his cargos and extracts a plastic bag. In it is a mobile phone, with a Spanish SIM card. He calls Rubio, the Spaniard who will drive him north to Catalonia.

"Soy Murad. El amigo de Rahal."

"Espéreme por la caña de azúcar."

"Bien."

He takes a few steps forward, but he doesn't see the sugar cane Rubio mentioned. He continues walking anyway. A hotel appears on the horizon. Another dog barks, and the sound soon turns into a howl. He walks toward it and spots the sugar cane. A small path appears on the left side and he sits at its end. He takes his shoes off, curls his frigid toes in the wet socks and massages them. Replacing his shoes, he lies back and takes a deep breath of relief. He can't believe his luck. He made it.

It will be all right now. He comforts himself with the familiar fantasy that sustained him back home, all those nights when he couldn't fall asleep, worrying about how he would pay rent or feed his mother and brothers. He imagines the office where he'll be working; he can see his fingers moving quickly and precisely over his keyboard; he can hear his phone ringing. He pictures himself going home to a modern, well-furnished apartment, his wife greeting him, the TV in the background.

A light shines on him. Rubio is fast. No wonder it cost so much to hire him. Murad sits up. The light is away from his eyes only a moment, but it is long enough to see the dog, a German shepherd, and the infinitely more menacing form holding the leash.

THE OFFICER FROM the Guardia Civil wears fatigues, and a black beret cocked over his shaved head. His name tag reads Martinez. He sits inside the van with Murad and the other illegals, the dog at his feet. Murad looks at himself: his wet shoes, his dirty pants stuck against his legs, the bluish skin under his nails. He keeps his teeth clenched to stop himself from shivering beneath the blanket the officer gave him. It's only fourteen kilometers, he thinks. If they hadn't been forced into the water, if he'd swum faster, if he'd gone west instead of east, he would have made it.

When he climbs down from the van, Murad notices a wooded area up the hill just a few meters away, and beyond it, a road. The guards are busy helping a woman who seems to have collapsed from the cold. Murad takes off, running as fast as he can. Behind him, he hears a whistle and the sound of boots, but he continues running, through the trees, his feet barely touching the crackled ground. When he gets closer to the road, he sees it is a four-lane highway, with cars whizzing by. It makes him pause. Martinez grabs him by the shirt.

THE CLOCK ON THE WALL at the Guardia Civil post shows six in the morning. Murad sits on a metal chair, handcuffed. There are men and women, all wrapped in blankets like him, huddled close together to stay warm. He doesn't recognize many of them; most came on other boats. Scarface sits alone, smoking a cigarette, one leg resting on the other, one shoe missing. There is no sign of Aziz. He must have made it. Just to be sure, he asks the

Guinean woman a few seats down from him. "I haven't seen him," she says.

Lucky Aziz. Murad curses his own luck. If he'd landed just a hundred meters west, away from the houses and the hotel, he might have been able to escape. His stomach growls. He swallows hard. How will he be able to show his face again in Tangier? He stands up and hobbles to the dusty window. He sees Faten outside, her head bare, in a line with some of the other boatmates, waiting for the doctors, who wear surgical masks on their faces, to examine them. A wave of relief washes over him, and he gesticulates as best as he can with his handcuffs, calling her name. She can't hear him, but eventually she looks up, sees him, then looks away.

A woman in a dark business suit arrives, her high heels clicking on the tiled floor. "Soy sus abogada," she says, standing before them. She tells them they are here illegally and that they must sign the paper that the Guardia Civil are going to give them. While everyone takes turns at signing, the woman leans against the counter to talk to one of the officers. She raises one of her legs behind her as she talks, like a little girl. The officer says something in a flirtatious tone, and she throws her head back and laughs.

Murad puts in a false name even though it won't matter. He is taken to the holding station, the sand from the beach still stuck on his pants. On his way there, he sees a body bag on the ground. A sour taste invades his mouth. He swallows but can't contain it. He doubles over and the officer lets go of him. Murad stumbles to the side of the building and vomits. It could have been him in that body bag; it could have been Faten. Maybe it was Aziz or Halima.

The guard takes him to a moldy cell already occupied by two other prisoners, one of whom is asleep on the mattress. Murad sits on the floor and looks up through the window at the patch of blue sky. Seagulls flutter from the side of the building and fly away in formation, and for a moment he envies them their freedom. But tomorrow the police will send him back to Tangier. His future there stands before him, unalterable, despite his efforts, despite the risk he took and the price he paid. He will have to return to the same old apartment, to live off his mother and sister, without any prospects or opportunity. He thinks of Aziz, probably already on a truck headed to Catalonia, and he wonders—if Aziz can make it, why not he? At least now he knows what to expect. It will be hard to convince his mother, but in the end he knows he will prevail on her to sell her gold bracelets. If she sells all seven of them, it will pay for another trip. And next time, he'll make it.

PART 1:

Before

The Fanatic

LARBI AMRANI DIDN'T consider himself a superstitious man, but when the prayer beads that hung on his rearview mirror broke, he found himself worrying that this could be an omen. His mother had given him the sandalwood beads on his college graduation, shortly before her death, advising him to use them often. At first Larbi had carried the beads in his pocket, fingered them after every prayer, but as the years went by he'd reached for them with decreasing regularity, until one day they ended up as decoration in his car. Now they lay scattered, amber dots on the black floor mats. He picked up as many as he could find and put them in the cup holder, hoping to get them fixed later. He eased the Mercedes down the driveway and into the quiet, tree-lined street. Traffic was unusually light, even when he passed through the crenellated fortress walls at Bab Rouah.

In his office at the Moroccan Ministry of Education, he opened up the day's *Al-Alam* and asked the chaouch to bring him a glass of mint tea. In a few minutes he would tackle another pile of dossiers, deciding where newly graduated teachers would perform their two years of civil service, but for now he took his time reading the paper and sipping his tea. The headlines announced a train workers' strike and yet another hike in the prices of milk and flour, so he skipped to the sports page.

Before he could read the weekend football scores, his secretary buzzed him to announce that he had a visitor. Larbi put the paper away and stood up to welcome Si Tawfiq, an old friend he hadn't seen in fifteen years. (Or was it fourteen?) They had lived next door to each other in a new apartment complex in downtown Rabat, but after moving out to the suburbs they had lost touch. Si Tawfiq entered the room cloaked in his white burnous, even on this warm September day. After salaams and other pleasantries had been exchanged, Tawfiq cleared his throat. "It's about my niece. She's finishing her degree next summer." His protruding eyes, the result of a thyroid condition, made Larbi uncomfortable.

"Congratulations," Larbi said.

"And she wants a job in Rabat." Tawfiq smiled knowingly.

Larbi tried to conceal his annoyance. The greatest need for teachers was in smaller towns and in the forgotten villages of the Atlas Mountains.

"I was hoping you could help her," Tawfiq added.

"I wish I could, Si Tawfiq," Larbi began. "But we have so few jobs in the city these days. The waiting list is this thick." He held his fingers wide apart, as if he were talking about the phone book.

"I understand," Tawfiq said. "Of course, we would try to do anything we could to help you."

Larbi stroked the ends of his thin mustache, twisting them upward. He was not above taking the occasional bribe, but he recalled the morning's omen. "Please," he said, holding up his palms. "There's no need." He cleared his throat and added weakly, "I'm happy to serve all teachers. It's just that when so many people want the same thing, it becomes impossible to get all of them the assignment they want."

Tawfiq looked disappointed, and he stared at Larbi for a long minute. "I understand," he said. "That's why I've come to you."

Larbi sighed. He didn't want to disappoint his friend,

and anyway, what sense did it make to refuse a favor to a department head in the Sureté Nationale? "I'll see what I can do," he said. Moving Tawfiq's niece up the list would require creative handling of the paperwork. He'd have to be discreet.

Afterward, Larbi swiveled in his chair and put his feet on the desk, crossing them at the ankles. He looked out the window at the row of eucalyptus trees outside and thought again about his mother, her benevolent face appearing in his mind's eye. He lit a Marlboro and inhaled slowly. Times were different now. He didn't create the system; he was just getting by, like everyone else. He turned to face his pile of dossiers.

WHEN LARBI GOT HOME that night, there was a nice surprise waiting for him on the console—a rare letter from his son, Nadir, who was studying electrical engineering in Québec. Larbi stepped inside the living room and sat on one of the leather sofas, moving a white-and-pink silk cushion out of the way. Two years ago, Larbi's daughter, Noura, had taken up silk painting and, besides cushions, had made scarves, handkerchiefs, and watercolors. The results of her labor were scattered around the house. Larbi had thought that she'd taken a serious inter-

est in decorative arts, but it turned out to be nothing more
than a high school fad, and all the brushes and bottles of
paints she'd insisted on buying were now in a plastic bag
somewhere under the kitchen sink.

Larbi opened the letter. These days, Nadir sent only
hurried e-mails with scant details of college life. Whenever
he wrote real letters, it was to ask his parents for money.
This one was no different—he wanted 10,000 dirhams to
buy a new laptop. Larbi shook his head. Nadir would
probably spend it on CDs or a weekend out of town. But
he didn't mind, so long as the boy did well in school, and
he always did. Larbi loved to think of his son's future and
of the position Nadir would be able to get with an engineering degree, especially one from abroad.

Larbi walked through the corridor to Noura's room.
He thought for a moment that she wasn't home, because
her stereo wasn't blaring rock music, as it usually did, but
he heard voices and so he knocked. Noura opened the
door. She wore jeans and a black T-shirt with glittery letters spelling out the name of a rock band. Her hair fell in
curly cascades on her shoulders. She looked at her watch.
"It's already six-thirty?" she said, sounding surprised.

"Look what I got for you," Larbi said, handing her
some magazines he'd bought on his way home.

"Thanks, Papa," Noura said. She took the magazines from him, and when she stepped aside to drop them on her desk he saw her friend, a girl who sat on the chair by the window, her hands folded on her lap. She wore a gray, pilled sweater and an ankle-length denim skirt, and her hair was covered in a headscarf. Noura introduced her as Faten Khatibi, one of her classmates at the university in Rabat. Noura was supposed to have gone to NYU, but her scores on the standardized TOEFL exam were not high enough, and so she had to take a year of English at the public university. She was going to apply again in December. The delay had left her somewhat depressed, and the feeling was compounded by her loneliness—most of her friends from the private French lycée she'd attended had gone on to universities abroad.

Larbi stepped into the room and cheerfully extended his hand to Faten, but Faten didn't take it. "Pardon me," she said. Her eyes shifted back to Noura and she smiled. Larbi dropped his hand awkwardly by his side. "Well." There was unpleasant pause; Larbi could think of nothing to say. "I'll leave you two alone."

As he went toward the kitchen to get a drink, Larbi heard the key turn in the lock. His wife, Salma, walked in, her leather satchel on one arm and a set of laundered shirts on the other. "Sorry I'm late," she said. "The judge took a long recess." Larbi took the shirts from her, dropping them on a chair in the foyer. He asked her who Noura's friend was. Salma shrugged. "Someone she met at school."

"She's not the type of girl I've seen her with before."

"You mean she's not an enfant gatée?" Salma gave him a little ironic smile. She had little patience with Noura's friends, private-school kids who spent most of their time worrying about their clothes or their cars. Years ago, Salma had disapproved of the idea of Noura's going to a French school, and Larbi himself had occasionally felt guilty that his own daughter was not part of the school system he helped to administer. Yet he had insisted; his daughter had so much potential, and he wanted her to succeed. Surely even an idealist like Salma could understand that.

"I just don't want her to mix with the wrong type," he said.

"She'll be fine," Salma said, giving him that woman-of-the-people look she affected from time to time and which irritated him supremely—just because she took on several cases every year for free and was active in the Moroccan Association of Human Rights didn't mean she knew any better than Larbi.

• • •

FATEN BECAME A REGULAR visitor in Larbi's home. He grew accustomed to seeing her hooded figure in the corridor and her shoes with their thick, curled soles outside Noura's door. Now that Noura spent so much time with her, Larbi watched Sunday-afternoon football matches by himself. This week his beloved Raja of Rabat were playing their archrivals, the Widad of Casablanca. Salma, for whom football was only slightly more exciting than waiting for a pot of tea to brew, went to take a nap. When Larbi went to the kitchen at halftime to get a beer, he heard Faten's voice. "The injustice we see every day," she said, "is proof enough of the corruption of King Hassan, the government, and the political parties. But if we had been better Muslims, perhaps these problems wouldn't have been visited on our nation and on our brethren elsewhere."

"What do you mean?" Noura asked.

"Only by purifying our thoughts and our actions . . ."

Larbi walked a few steps down the hallway to Noura's open door, which she promptly closed when she saw him. He retreated to the living room, where he smoked his Marlboros, drank more beer, and barely paid any attention to the rest of the match.

Immediately after Faten's departure, Larbi knocked on Noura's door to ask what their conversation had been about. He stood close to her, and she wrinkled her nose when he spoke. His breath smelled of alcohol, he realized, and he stepped back.

"Nothing, Papa," she said.

"How can you say 'nothing'? She was here for a while."

"We were just talking about problems at school, that sort of thing." She turned around and, standing over her desk, stacked a few notebooks.

Larbi stepped in. "What problems?"

Noura gave him a surprised look, shrugged, then busied herself with inserting a few CDs in their cases. On the wall above her desk was a silk painting of a peony, its leaves open and languid, its center white and pink. Larbi stood, waiting. "She was just telling me how last year some students didn't even sit for final exams, but they passed. I guess they bribed someone on the faculty."

"What would she know of such things?" asked Larbi, frowning.

Noura heaved a sigh. "She has firsthand experience. She flunked last year."

"Maybe she didn't work hard enough."

Noura looked up at him and said in a tone that made it clear that she wanted him to leave after this, "The kids who passed didn't, either."

"She can't blame her failure on others."

Noura pulled her hair up into a ponytail. She took out a pair of lounging pants and a T-shirt from her marble-top dresser, flung them on the bed, and stood, arms akimbo, waiting. "I need to take a shower now." Larbi scrutinized his daughter's face, but it was as impassive as a plastic mask. He left the room.

Salma was still napping when he entered their bedroom. He sat on the bed, facing her. Her eyelids fluttered. Without waiting for her to fully awaken, Larbi said, "Noura can't see this girl anymore."

"What?" Salma said, opening her eyes. "What are you talking about?" She was already frowning, as though she was ready to analyze the situation and construct the right argument.

"I don't think it's a good idea. I caught them talking politics just now."

"So?"

"Don't give me that look of yours, Salma. You know exactly what I mean. I don't want her involved in anything. If someone heard them talking that way about the king at school, there could be trouble."

Salma sighed and got up. "I think Faten is good for her, frankly. Noura needs to know what's going on around her."

"What do you mean?"

"The world doesn't revolve around fashion and movies."

"She can look around for herself! What does she need this girl for?"

"Look, Noura's going to be leaving at the end of the school year anyway, so I doubt they're going to see each other after that." Salma adjusted her dress and tightened her belt. "You're making a mountain out of a seed," she said. She was the sort of woman who liked to end discussions with a proverb.

Larbi shook his head.

"By the way," Salma said. "You won't believe who called this morning. Si Tawfiq, remember him?"

"Of course," Larbi said, getting up. He had already made up his mind to help him with his niece's situation. "I'll give him a call back."

AS WEEKS WENT BY, Noura seemed to be increasingly absorbed by her books. One Saturday afternoon in October, Larbi asked her if she wanted to go to the theater. The performance was by a stand-up comic who'd been banned for a few years and only recently allowed to perform again. The show was sold out. He thought it would be good if she took a break from all that studying.

"I have to write an essay," she said. The soft sound of Qur'anic chanting wafted from her CD player.

"You're missing out," Larbi replied. This wasn't the first time Noura had declined an outing. The week before, she had turned down an invitation to go to a tennis finals match, and two weeks before that she had refused to join them at the betrothal of her second cousin. She had always been a good student, but he didn't understand why she worked so hard now. This was supposed to be an easy year, to improve her English. There would be plenty of time to study next year in New York. "Come on," he said. "Spend some time with your father for a change."

"Fine, Baba," Noura said.

On the way to the theater, Larbi glanced at Noura in the rearview mirror. "You're not wearing makeup," he observed.

Salma laughed. "Don't tell me you cared for her eyeliner."

"I'm just saying. It's the theater, after all."

"Why should I paint my face to please other people?" Noura said indignantly.

Salma pulled down the passenger-side mirror and stared at her daughter in it. "I thought you liked to do it for yourself."

Noura bit at her unmanicured nails, tilting her head in a way that could have meant yes as much as no, then shrugged.

The comedian's routine was a mix of biting satire and musical numbers, but although everyone around him laughed, Larbi found he couldn't relax. He wanted to talk to Noura, though he feared she would again say it was nothing.

The next day, Larbi waited for his daughter to leave for school before slipping into her room, unsure what to look for. The windows were open and the sun was making tree spots on the floor. Larbi sat on his daughter's bed. It struck him that it was made, the crocheted cover pulled neatly on all sides. She had always been messy, and he'd often joked that he'd need a compass to find his way out of her room. Now he felt silly for finding her sudden neatness suspicious. Salma was right, he worried for no reason. He got up to leave, but the garish color of a paperback on the nightstand caught his eye and he reached for it. It was a book on political Islam. Leafing through it, he saw that the print quality was poor and that the text was littered with typographical errors. How could Noura bother with this? He tossed it back on the nightstand, where it hit another tome, this one a leather-bound volume. Larbi tilted his head sideways to read the spine. It was *Ma'alim fi Ttariq* by Sayyid Qutb, the Egyptian dissident and member of the Muslim Brotherhood. He doubted that Noura, who'd been schooled at Lycée Descartes, could even read the complicated classical Arabic in a book like that, but its presence on her nightstand made him look frantically around the room for other clues. Next to her stereo he found a stack of tapes, and when he played one it turned out to be a long commentary on jurisprudence, peppered with brief diatribes about the loose morals of young people. He couldn't find anything else out of the ordinary.

When Noura came home for lunch he was waiting for her in the living room. "What's this?" he asked, holding up the Sayyid Qutb book.

"You were looking through my things?" Noura said, looking surprised and hurt.

"Listen to me. I'll only say this once. You're not to see this girl Faten any longer."

"Why?"

"I don't like what she's doing to you."

"What is she doing to me, Baba?"

"I don't want that girl in my house anymore. Safi!"

Noura gave him a dark look, turned on her heel, and left the room. When the maid served lunch, Noura said she wasn't hungry. Larbi didn't mind. Better a sulking child than one who gets in trouble.

IT WAS ONLY A few weeks later, the day before Ramadan, that Noura made her announcement. Salma was shuffling back and forth from the kitchen, where the maid was roasting sesame seeds in the oven for the briwat pastries she would make for the holy month. Larbi was looking at pictures Nadir had sent of the apartment he'd just moved into with a friend, and he was more amused than upset to see no trace of the laptop the boy had claimed he needed.

"You're spoiling him," Salma said.

"He's going to get a master's degree," Larbi replied.

Noura walked into the dining room and sat down at the breakfast table. "I've decided to start wearing the hijab." Salma reached for her daughter's hand and knocked over her cup of coffee. She pushed her chair away from the table and used her napkin to blot the stained tablecloth.

"What? Why?" Larbi asked, dropping the pictures on the table.

"Because God commands us to do so. It says so in the Qur'an," Noura replied.

"Since when do you quote from the Qur'an?" he said, forcing himself to smile.

"There are only two verses that refer to the headscarf. You should take them in context," her mother argued.

"Don't you believe that the Qur'an is the word of God?" Noura asked.

"Of course we do," said Larbi, "but those were different times."

"If you disagree with the hijab, you're disagreeing with God," she said.

The confident tone in her voice scared him. "And you have a direct phone line to God, do you?" he said.

Salma raised her hand to stop Larbi. "What has gotten into you?" she asked her daughter. Noura looked down. She traced the intricate geometric pattern on the red rug with her big toe. "Those verses refer to modesty," Salma continued. "And besides, those were the pagan times of jahiliya, not the twenty-first century."

"God's commandments are true for all time," Noura replied, her brow furrowed. "And in some ways, we're still living in jahiliya." Larbi and Salma glanced at each other. Noura drew her breath again. "Women are harassed on the streets in Rabat all the time. The hijab is a protection."

Salma opened her mouth to respond, but no sound emerged. Larbi knew that his wife was thinking of those young men with hungry eyes, of how they whistled when they saw a pretty girl and how they never teased the ones with headscarves. "So what?" Larbi said, his voice already loud. He stood up. "The men can't behave, so now my daughter has to cover herself? They're supposed to avert their eyes. That's in the Qur'an, too, you know."

"I don't understand why it's a problem," Noura said. "This is between me and God." She got up as well, and they stared at each other across the table. At last Noura left the dining room.

Larbi was in shock. His only daughter, dressed like some ignorant peasant! But even peasants didn't dress like that. She wasn't talking about wearing some traditional country outfit. No, she wanted the accoutrements of the new breed of Muslim Brothers: headscarf tightly folded around her face, severe expression anchored in her eyes. His precious daughter. She would look like those rabble-rousers you see on live news channels, eyes darting, mouths agape, fists raised. But, he tried to tell himself, maybe this was just a fleeting interest, maybe it would all go away. After all, Noura had had other infatuations. She had been a rabid antismoking advocate. She'd thrown his cigarettes

away when he wasn't looking, cut pictures of lungs dark
with tar out of books and taped them to the refrigerator.
Eventually she gave up and let him be. She'd also had a
string of hobbies that she took up with astonishing passion
and then abandoned a few months later for no apparent
reason—jewelry making, box collecting, the flute, sign
language. But what if this was different? What if he lost
her to this . . . this blindness that she thought was sight?

He thought about the day, a long time ago now, when
he'd almost lost her. She was only two. They had gone to
the beach in Temara for the day, and Nadir had asked for
ice cream. Larbi had called out to one of the vendors who
walked back and forth on the beach. He'd paid for the
cones and handed one to Salma and one to Nadir, but
when he'd turned around to give Noura hers, he realized
she'd vanished. They'd looked for her for hours. He remembered his face burning in the sun, the vein at the base
of his neck throbbing with fear and worry, his feet swelling
from walking on the sand. He remembered the tears that
continued to stream down Salma's face as they searched
the beach. Eventually an old woman brought the disori-
ented toddler to the police station. Noura had gone to collect seashells, and it took the old woman a while to realize
that the girl who had sat quietly on the rocks was alone.

He'd promised himself then never to lose sight of her, but the terror he felt that day came rushing in, and the weight of it made him sit down in his chair, his head in his hands.

Moments later, Larbi heard Noura's footsteps in the corridor. He could see her in front of the mirror, her freckled face turned to the light coming from the living room, placing a scarf on her head, tying it under her chin so that her hair was fully covered. Before he could think about what he was doing, he lunged at her and took off the scarf. Noura let out a cry. Salma stood up at the dining table but didn't come to her daughter's rescue.

"What are you doing?" Noura cried.

"You're not going out like that." Larbi threw the scarf on the floor.

"You can't stop me!"

Larbi didn't say anything. He knew that she was right, of course, that he couldn't keep her under lock and key just because she wanted to dress like half the city's female population. Noura picked up her scarf and quietly resumed tying it on her head. She said her good-byes and left. Larbi turned to look at his wife, whose face displayed the same stunned expression as when Noura had first spoken.

ON THE FIRST NIGHT of Ramadan, Salma took out her best china and set the table herself. She had sent the maid home to celebrate with her own family. One by one, she brought forth the dishes they had prepared that day: harira soup with lamb, beghrir smothered with honey, sesame shebbakiya, dates stuffed with marzipan, and a tray of assorted nuts. Larbi called out to Noura that it was time to eat, then sat down to await the adhan of the muezzin, the moment when day became dusk, the fast would end, and they could eat. At last, Noura poked her head in and stood listlessly at the entrance of the dining room. Larbi looked at her beautiful hair, its loose curls reaching her chest. It was a reminder of what she had chosen to do.

The TV announcer came on to say that the sun was setting; the call for prayer resonated immediately after. Salma gestured to Noura. "Sit, so we can eat."

"I'll only break the fast with water. I'll eat after I've done the maghrib prayer."

Salma glanced at Larbi. "Fine," he said.

Noura added, "We're supposed to have frugal meals during Ramadan, not this orgy of food." She pointed to the festive table her mother had prepared.

Larbi felt his appetite melt away. Instead, he craved a cigarette and a stiff drink. Preferably Scotch. Of course, there wasn't a place in the city that would sell alcohol for another twenty-nine days. He swallowed with difficulty. It was going to be a long Ramadan. "We'll wait for you," he said.

Noura turned to leave, but then turned back. "Well, maybe just a little bit of shebbakiya," she said. She took a healthy bite out of the candy.

"Didn't you say this was too much food?" Salma asked.

The family ate without talking. In years past, this first night had been special; friends and family would sit around the table, sharing stories of their fast and enjoying their meal, but there had been too much on Larbi's mind lately to think about inviting anyone.

IT WAS YET another drought year—the end of November and no rainfall at all. Looking at his desk calendar, Larbi noticed that the NYU application deadline was approaching. At least he had Noura's future to look forward to, he thought, even if the present was difficult. Since she had taken on the hijab, he had stopped mentioning her at work. He felt it was beneath someone like him to have a daughter in a headscarf, and he provided only terse answers to anyone at the Ministry who asked him about his daughter.

After work he found her in her room with her mother, busy hanging new curtains. He asked her if he could read her essay before she sent it out.

"I'm not applying," she replied. She slid the last curtain tab onto a mahogany pole.

Larbi glared at her. "Why not?"

"Because I want to transfer out of university at the end of next year. I'm going to be a middle school teacher."

"What happened to your plans to study economics?" Salma asked, sitting down.

"Morocco needs me. You two always talk about the shortage of teachers," Noura said.

"Have you lost your mind? You're not going to solve the shortage problem—"

"Am I crazy to want to help my country?" She turned away and climbed onto her desk to place the pole on the brackets.

"Look, you'll be of more help as an economist than as a schoolteacher," Larbi said. "It's that friend of hers," he added, turning to his wife. "She's filled her head with these ideas and now she can't think for herself."

"No one is filling my head," Noura said, standing next to the window, the late afternoon light in her hair. "There's too much corruption in the system now, and I want to be

a part of the solution." Larbi wondered if she was refer-
ring to him. No, that was impossible. He had always kept
his deals secret from his wife and daughter. Still, he thought
it best not to respond. Noura jumped down from the desk.
"Besides, why go to school in the States when I can just as
easily study here?"

"For the experience, child," said Salma.

"And you think people in America are going to want
me?" Noura said, raising her voice. "Americans hate us."

"How would you know if you've never been there?"
Salma asked. "Your brother has never complained. Why
don't you talk to him?"

"He's in Canada," Noura spat, as though her mother
couldn't tell the difference.

"Doesn't your Islam tell you to listen to your father?"
Larbi asked.

"Only if my father is on the right path."

"Congratulations, then. You alone are on the right
path," he said.

"Baraka!" Salma said. She got up. "What about all
those years you spent learning English? All the plans you
had?"

"I really want to be a teacher," Noura said.

"Think carefully about what you're doing, ya Noura.

People your age would do anything for an opportunity like this, and you squander it."

"I want to stay," Noura said, and she pulled the new curtains shut.

IT WAS SALMA's idea to invite Faten to dinner. Larbi had agreed, reluctantly at first, then resignedly, thinking that perhaps he might be able to talk some sense into his daughter if he understood her friend a little better. It was a Saturday evening, and the table had been set with a new service Salma had bought. Larbi sat at the head of the table with Noura to his left. Salma sat to his right, under the framed silhouette of a younger version of herself. During their honeymoon in Paris some twenty-five years ago, they had gone to Montmartre, where an artist had talked them into getting their silhouettes done. Working with his scissors, the old man had made Salma's bust more generous, and she'd laughed and left him a good tip.

Faten sat across from Larbi, at the other end of the table, looking calm and content. She had amber-colored eyes, plump lips, and skin so fair that it seemed as though all the light in the room converged upon it. She was, in other words, beautiful. This maddened Larbi. God is beautiful, and He loves beauty, so why hide it beneath all that cloth?

The maid brought the main dish, a stew of chicken with black olives and preserved lemons. "Thank you, um . . ." Faten said, looking up.

"Mimouna," the maid said, glancing at Larbi.

"Thank you, Mimouna," Faten said.

"To your health," Mimouna replied, smiling.

Larbi started to eat, periodically glancing at Faten. He was mildly satisfied to notice evidence of less-than-genteel upbringing—she had placed her knife back on the table even after using it. After a decent amount of time had been spent eating and the expected compliments had been made about the food, Larbi cleared his throat. "How old are you, my child?" he asked, affecting as gentle a tone as he could muster toward the girl.

"Nineteen," Faten replied.

"Noura told me you're repeating this year," he said.

Noura shot her father an exasperated look.

"That's true," Faten said.

"I was sorry to hear that. It must have been tough."

Noura slammed her fork on the side of her plate and dropped her chin in her hand. She stared at her father angrily.

Salma intervened. "And are you from Rabat?" she asked Faten in a pleasant tone.

"I was born here, but I grew up in Agadir. I've been back only four years now."

"So where do your parents live?" asked Larbi.

"I live with my mother." Faten's voice dropped an octave. "In Douar Lhajja."

Salma picked up the bread basket and offered it to Faten. "Have some more," she said.

"Let me ask you something," Larbi said. "If someone offered you a chance to study in New York, would you take it?"

"Not again," Noura sighed. Yet she seemed interested in what her friend would say, for she turned and waited for an answer.

Faten blinked. "No one is offering me anything."

"But if someone did."

"I would want to know why they made the offer. No one gives anything for free. That is the trouble with some of our youths."

Larbi felt a lecture coming from Faten, and so he called the maid to ask for more water. Mimouna brought another bottle of water and refilled Faten's glass, but she left without refilling Larbi's. "What do you plan to do after graduation?" he asked Faten.

"I'm not sure yet. It's all in God's hands."

"My daughter here wants to leave school, give up going to NYU, and go teach in the villages."

Faten smiled with approbation. "She will do a lot of good."

"Don't you think that a degree from abroad would be better for her?"

"No, I don't. I think it's a shame that we always value foreign degrees over ours. We're so blinded by our love for the West that we're willing to give them our brightest instead of keeping them here where we need them."

"If you think teaching middle school is so good, why don't you join Noura?" Larbi asked.

"I may well do that," Faten said cheerfully, "although, to tell the truth, I'm not very good with children." The dismissive wave of her hand as she spoke made Larbi's heart sink. He was losing control of his daughter to this girl, who didn't even seem to care enough to want to go with her. Faten pushed her plate away. "You must be so proud," she said. Of all the things she could have said, this made Larbi angriest. He didn't say anything for the rest of the meal, rudely getting up from the table before the tea was served.

He was outside smoking cigarettes when Salma slid the glass doors open and joined him on the terrace. She sat on the wrought-iron chair next to him, and they stared at the blooming jacaranda trees that lined the far end of the backyard. Salma spoke at last. "What are you going to do about this?" There was a hint of accusation in her tone that made Larbi want to scream.

"*Now* you want something done?" he asked.

"I didn't know it was going to get to this."

Larbi pulled on his cigarette. "What do you think I should do, then, a lalla?"

"I don't know. Just do something," Salma said.

He didn't have the heart to tell her that he'd already asked Si Tawfiq for help, and that his friend had said there were no police records on Faten. She was a member of the Islamic Student Organization, but the investigation hadn't turned up anything illegal. Tawfiq said he'd keep an eye on her. All they could do now was wait.

MONTHS WENT BY. Exam season was a busy time at the Ministry, so when Si Raouf rang the doorbell at the house, Larbi thought it was because of some work matter and he hoped to settle it fast and have him leave before the subject of Noura came up. Larbi knew Si Raouf from his days as an education inspector. Raouf had been a schoolteacher, but eventually he had finished his Ph.D. and now he was a lecturer at Noura's college. Today Raouf had the exhausted look he always had this time of year, when he had to grade hundreds of undergraduate papers. The maid served the tea, but neither man touched his glass.

"It's Noura, Si Larbi," Raouf said, his eyes looking intermittently away, his voice tinged with nervousness. "She passed a note to someone."

Larbi felt his stomach tighten. "I-I don't understand," he whispered.

"One of the students—Faten Khatibi is her name—she passed a paper to Noura with questions and Noura sent her back the answers."

"She cheated?" Salma sounded incredulous.

"She helped someone cheat," Raouf said, in an effort to lessen the blow. "This is grounds for expulsion. But we're friends, and I thought I'd warn you. If it happens again with another proctor, there could be a problem."

Larbi walked the professor out. Then he turned around, marched to Noura's room, and flung open the door without knocking. Noura was at her desk. He grabbed her by the arm. She stood.

"Cheating at the exams? This is how you repay us after all the sacrifices we've made for you?" Larbi said.

"W-what?"

"How will I ever be able to show my face at the Ministry?" he shouted. "My own daughter is caught cheating at the exams!"

"I was just trying to help Faten. She didn't know the answers—"

"Help her? You think this is a word game?" Salma asked. "You didn't help. You cheated."

"I-I couldn't say no. She begged me."

"You lecture us about right and wrong and then you cheat at your exams. Have you ever opened the Holy Book or do you get everything secondhand from Faten?" Salma asked.

"If I ever hear one more word about that damn girl, by God, I'll lock you up in your room," Larbi said. "I won't have a word said about my reputation, do you hear me?"

"Everybody cheats. Everybody." Noura looked him straight in the eye, and he couldn't hold her stare. He'd always kept the favors he did for his friends quiet, but now he suspected that she knew somehow.

"That doesn't make it right," Salma said.

Noura disappeared in her room for two days after that, reappearing only to watch a TV program on religion and jurisprudence called *Ask the Mufti*. She'd never missed an episode. She would come in and sit in the family room when the program was on, her eyes riveted on the screen. People phoned in with various questions, from the serious ("What is the proper way of calculating the zakat alms?") to the simple ("How do I complete the pilgrimage?"), and Noura watched it all. Today someone phoned in to ask,

"Is the use of mouthwash permissible even though it contains alcohol?" Noura looked at the old mufti with great anticipation. Salma abruptly took hold of the remote control and changed channels. When Noura called out in surprise, Salma said, "I can't believe you're interested in silly details about mouthwash when you can't even see anything wrong with cheating at exams." Larbi laughed, but he was overcome by bitterness. If only he could get that damn girl away from his daughter, perhaps he might be able to convince Noura to go visit her aunt in Marrakech—a stay in the southern city might do her some good. But first he had to deal with Faten once and for all. He picked up the phone. The exams were still being scored, and there was still time to act. He needed someone trustworthy to deal with Faten, and he knew Raouf would not let him down.

LARBI SAT AT HIS wife's vanity, trimming his mustache, while Salma folded the laundry. He suddenly felt nostalgic and wanted to ask her about those heady days in the seventies when they were both young and the world was open before them and they had big dreams of setting it right. He had started out as an educator and she as a lawyer, but while she still spent her days trying to help clients, he had moved on to administrative positions and had been unable to resist the temptations that came with them. What had happened to him, he wanted to ask. He felt he had failed, though he didn't know when that had happened. He heard a knock on the door. It was Noura. "I passed my exams," she announced, smiling.

"Mbarek u messud," Salma said flatly, then resumed folding the clothes. Normally, she would have hugged Noura; she would have put her hand around her upper lip and let out several joy-cries, but now she sounded no happier than if her daughter had told her she'd successfully hung a painting.

"Baba, I have a favor to ask," Noura said. Larbi put down his scissors and turned to face her. "There's been a problem. Faten flunked her exams . . ." Her voice trailed off.

"And?" Larbi asked, unsurprised.

"Well, she already flunked them last year, so this means she's expelled now. She doesn't know what she's going to do."

Salma stood, hanger in hand, and pointed it at Noura. "Where are you going with this?" she asked.

"What's going to become of her? There are so many unemployed college graduates, but without a diploma, her chances of ever finding a job . . . It's so unfair—"

"I don't understand what that has to do with me," Larbi said.

"I thought perhaps you could sort it out. You have connections, and she asked me to see if you could help out," Noura said. Her eyes shifted away from him for a moment and then settled on him again.

Larbi smiled bitterly. Here she was, the purist, the hard-liner, the anticorruption activist, but in the end, she wanted her friend to get special treatment, just like everyone else. "No more talk of meritocracy?" he asked. Noura looked down. He paused to savor the moment, however fleeting he knew it would be. How many times had she rebuffed him when he asked her to take that damn scarf off and go back to the way she was? What of his dream to see her in cap and gown at NYU? His heart ached just to think of it. Now it was her turn to be on the asking end. "I don't think it'll be possible. It would require breaking the law. Utterly un-Islamic, as you well know," he said.

"When you play with fire, you get burned," Salma said as she closed the wardrobe doors. Noura stared at her angrily and then left the room.

Larbi turned around on the stool and looked at his reflection in the mirror for a while. He, too, had played with fire, but maybe he'd already been burned. When he reached for the scissors again, he noticed a velvet pouch tossed in the middle of the perfume bottles. He took it in his hand and opened it. In it were the prayer beads that had broken, years ago, it seemed, and which Salma had saved here for him. He couldn't help but think about his mother, for whom virtue and religion went hand in hand, about a time when he, too, believed that such a pairing was natural.

"I know I shouldn't be happy about someone's misery," Salma said. "But I'm glad Faten was expelled. At least now Noura won't be seeing as much of her at school."

Where had he gone wrong? He had always had Noura's best interests at heart. What was so bad about her life before? She had it all, and she was happy. Why did she have to turn to religion? Perhaps it was his absences from home, his fondness for the drink, or maybe it was all the bribes he took. It could be any of these things. He was at fault somehow. Or it could be none of these things at all. In the end it didn't matter, he had lost her again, and this time he didn't dare hope for someone to return her to him.

"Do you think that'll help?" Larbi asked his wife.

Salma shook her head. "I don't know."

Bus Rides

THE DAY AFTER MAATI beat her with an extension cord, Halima Bouhamsa packed up some clothes and took the bus to her mother's house in Sidi Beliout, near the old medina of Casablanca. The cord had left bubbly welts on her arms and face, and she couldn't hide them under her housedress. She arrived at the door of the studio apartment, a packet of La Ménara tea in her hand as an offering, and stood for a moment, hesitant. Her mother wouldn't be happy to see her, but she couldn't think of anywhere else to go. She knocked.

"Again?" said her mother, Fatiha.

Halima didn't even nod. She walked past Fatiha and into the studio, where the smell of camphor balls from the previous week's cleaning lingered in the air. Stripes of sunlight came through the closed shutters, making a hazy grid on the bare floor. On the far wall was a sepia photograph of Halima's father, the only inheritance he had left behind after years of struggle with lung cancer. A portable TV sat in the corner, a gift from Halima's brothers, both emigrants to France. She dropped her bag on the floor and walked over to the narrow kitchen.

"What happened this time?" Fatiha asked.

"He drank the rent money." Halima took off her jellaba, revealing her paisley-print dress and the blue belt encircling her small waist. She was twenty-nine, but the dark patches on her face and the stoop in her shoulders made her look much older. She sat down on a stool and let her chin rest in her hands.

Fatiha lit the Butagaz and put a kettle on it. "The Lord is with those who are patient," she said.

Halima wondered whether all the Lord ever wanted from His people was patience. Hadn't she suffered long enough? She was sure that the Lord also wanted His people to be happy, but she couldn't come up with a stock expression as a retort, the way her mother always did.

The kettle whistled. Fatiha made a pot of mint tea and served it on the low, round table. Halima took her glass and cradled it in her chapped hands. "If I don't give him money for drinking, he steals it from me."

"A woman must know how to handle her husband," Fatiha said reproachfully. She sat down, her ample bottom spilling over the sides of her chair. "Look, I'm going to get you a little something from a new sorceress I went to the other day. Make sure you put it in Maati's food this time. He'll become like a ring on your finger. You can turn it any way you want."

"Your magic doesn't work."

"That's because you don't follow my directions."

"I want a divorce."

Fatiha slapped her hand on her thigh, spilling tea on the table. "Curse Satan," she said. "How are you going to feed the children?" She wiped off the spilled tea with a wet rag.

"I already do. Do you think they can be fed on what he gives me?"

Maati made a living driving a cab for a businessman uptown, but there was little of it left by the time his bar tab was paid. Halima had taken janitorial jobs two days a week and made extra money by selling embroidery to neighbors and friends. She looked at her mother with mixed defiance and expectation.

"Child, be patient with your man," Fatiha said. "Look what happened to Hadda." Hadda was Halima's neighbor in the Zenata shanty. Her husband had taken up with another woman but refused to divorce her. She'd gone to court, but he hadn't shown up at any of the hearings. "Now she lives alone. She's neither married, really, nor free to remarry."

"Better than living with the son of a whore."

"See? This is why he beats you. You talk back."

Halima heaved a loud sigh, but her mother was unfazed. Fatiha got up and wiped off the new microwave that her sons had brought her on their latest visit. She readjusted the embroidered doily that she kept on top.

"I'm not like Hadda," Halima said.

"That's right," Fatiha said. "You've got children."

Halima undid her hair and nervously tied it up in a knot. She refilled her mother's glass. "How much did that sorceress of yours want?"

"Fifteen hundred dirhams," Fatiha said.

Halima chuckled. "I might as well give Maati the money. I could buy my divorce from him."

"Even if you do," Fatiha said, "he won't let you have the children."

Halima gnawed at her thumb. "Then I'll bribe the judge,"

she said, her chin raised. She waited to see if her mother would say something, would discredit this idea as she had all the others.

Fatiha snorted. "You couldn't bribe a lowly clerk for that much."

Halima stared ahead of her, resisting the tears that she felt were coming.

"Let me take you to this sorceress," Fatiha said softly. "What do you have to lose?" Halima looked at her mother's face, at the sudden and gentle turn that her lips had taken, and wondered whom she should trust, the courts or the magicians.

IT TOOK SEVERAL WEEKS and another three beatings, the most recent only yesterday, before Halima managed to save the money to visit the sorceress her mother had recommended. She rode the bus back to Zenata and made it home in time to prepare the evening meal. She was going to make rghaif. The batter would be perfect for dissolving the pinch of powder that the sorceress had sold her. As Halima kneaded the dough, she heard the sound of the muezzins exhorting the faithful for the afternoon prayer. She winced at the thought of what she was about to do: a grave sin it was, the use of sorcerers. Nevertheless, the money was already spent, and if indeed actions were judged by one's niyyah, then she had already sinned by intending to use sorcery, so she might as well go through with it. As soon as the first rghifa was ready, she tasted it, burning her tongue in the process. The powder made it look yellowish, but the taste didn't appear to be altered. She grilled the rest of the rghaif and prepared a pot of tea, a strong one, with more tea and less mint, just the way Maati liked it.

She unhooked the clothes from the line in the courtyard and took them into the only bedroom, a dark, humid space without windows. She put them away in the armoire that was tipped against the naked cement wall because of its wobbly legs, straightening the sheet that separated her bed from the children's as she walked out. She went to the kitchen and rolled the round table on its edge, setting it down in the courtyard, between the divan and the car seats the children had rescued from the trash heap a few blocks down. When it rained, the family had to eat in the kitchen, elbow to elbow on the cane mat, but today it was sunny and they could eat their dinner by daylight. No need to use the gas lamp.

Halima's daughter, Mouna, was the first to come home, her braids swinging on both sides of her head as she pushed the metal door open. Halima caught her breath. With her high forehead and aquiline nose, Mouna looked so much like her father. Mouna asked if she could go to the neighbor's house for dinner. Halima slipped her arm around her daughter's waist. "Stay here with me," she said.

"Can we eat dinner now, then?" Mouna asked, in a whining tone.

"We have to wait for your father."

Mouna sighed, loudly, dramatically. The boys had gotten unruly—lately Farid had started talking back—but, Halima thought, Mouna was a good child, she would go far. She could have everything Halima had wanted for herself—if only the family could get out of the shantytown, with its dirty alleys where teenagers sniffed glue by day and roamed around in bands at night.

Mouna's younger brothers, Farid and Amin, walked in and dropped their schoolbags on the floor. The three children decided on a game of cards. "Don't cheat," warned Amin, the youngest. They sat on the ground in a patch of sunlight and started to play. Above them, flies danced in a never-ending circle.

For days after he beat Halima, Maati would sulk. Hours would go by, she'd wait for him to apologize or at least speak to her; but he never did, and she'd give up waiting and end up trying to console him, as though *he* were the one who'd been beaten. But tonight he came home with an apologetic look on his face. He let her sit on the divan with the children and took a car seat for himself, then served the tea. Halima watched as he ate his rghaif, finishing each one in only three bites. One thing that could be said for him was that he had a healthy appetite. If only he'd help out instead of drinking his money and eating hers. "These are delicious," he said, a smile on his face.

After dinner Halima cleared the table and sent the children to play outside. She was at the kitchen sink when Maati came up behind her, wrapping one arm around her shoulders. He kissed her neck and she felt it burn with heat. He still had that effect on her, even after ten years of marriage. When they had met at a neighbor's wedding, she'd immediately been attracted to his magnetic eyes, to his body, so thin yet full of pent-up energy. They had married only weeks later and had three children in four years before Halima went to the family planning clinic and got the Pill.

"Leave the dishes," he said. "You can do them later." He pulled her away from the sink, his hand on her wrist, and took her back to the courtyard, where they sat down on the divan. His skin felt softer than hers, yet his fingers had left a mark on her wrist where he had pulled her. He leaned in and kissed her palm. I shouldn't have doubted my mother, Halima thought. The powder is working.

THE NEXT DAY, Halima was waiting for the bus that would take her to the fish market at the Casablanca port, when she spotted a crisp fifty-dirham bill on the dusty sidewalk. What luck! That same morning, Maati had promised her he'd stop drinking and now this. When she got on the bus the attendant said he had an extra ticket that someone had bought by mistake and she could have it for ten rials. She smiled and put the ticket in her wallet. She found a seat by the window and looked at the outside world through the smudged glass. Buildings with peeling walls and satellite dishes flashed by, occasionally interrupted by palm trees.

At the market entrance, a one-eyed man in a dark brown jellaba sat on the ground, holding out his hand. He was so old that he could barely call out to passersby, his frail voice reaching only a few feet away. Halima looked through her wallet for some coins and gave them to him.

Along the lane, vendors in blue lab coats praised the freshness of their wares and their low prices. Halima stepped over the rivulets of fish scales and water that flowed between the stalls. Once a week she tried to break from the monotony of couscous, bean soups, and fritters that she could afford to feed the children by buying cheap fish. Ordinarily she would buy sardines or mackerel, but today she was in a mood to splurge, so after haggling with one of the vendors, she bought a large white fish for making a tagine.

While she worked on lunch, Halima found herself humming with Farid El-Atrache while he sang "Wayak" on the radio. She cleaned the fish over the sink, then cooked it in tomato and lemon sauce. The table was set, but Maati still wasn't home. She stood in her kitchen, trying to decide what to do. If she served the tagine now, the food would be cold by the time he got home and he might be upset. If she waited, the children would be late for school and he might still be upset. She hated these impossible choices that he forced her to make every day. She watched the clock with increasing anxiety, but soon she heard the creaking of the front door and grabbed the tagine and brought it out.

Maati sat cross-legged on the low divan, rubbing his hands together at the lemony smell emanating from the funnel-shape pot. The children sat around the table, and Halima took her seat, completing the circle. Maati cut the best pieces of fish and put them on the children's side of the communal dish. After getting a taste he said, "May God grant you health. This is excellent."

"To your health," she replied.

"The teacher said we need to buy a new history book," Farid said.

"Again?" Halima replied.

"Last time it was a grammar book, Mama," Farid said, rolling his eyes. Halima didn't know much about grammar or history, having taken only literacy classes, but she didn't like his tone.

"Tell her we'll buy it next week," Maati said. He tapped the boy's head, leaving a sticky imprint of fish sauce on it. Just a month earlier, Mouna had been unable to go with the rest of her class on a field trip to the Roman ruins at Volubilis, near Meknès. Halima knew that, despite his good intentions, Maati would not keep his promise to their child.

After the children had gone back to school, Maati and Halima settled down for tea. He was quiet today, but she didn't mind. She sat back on the divan, enjoying her drink. Maati finished his tea, then lay down to take a nap. "Aren't you going back to work?" she asked.

His eyes shifted. "The boss fired me."

Halima's heart jumped in her chest. She sat up. "Why?" she asked, even though she already knew that it must have been because he'd been caught drinking. She felt sorry for him, but disgust overcame pity. "Did you think Si Hussein would just let it slide?" Maati wrapped his arm across his forehead, shielding his eyes from her stare. "What are we going to do?" she asked.

"I'll find something else," he said. His tone was confident, but he turned his face away from her.

Halima glared at her husband. Mimicking his voice, she groaned, "I'll save money, I'll buy my own cab, I'll get us out of Zenata one day, you'll see." Maati took his arm off his eyes and looked at her. Halima stopped impersonating him. Still, she continued, "And all for what? We'll be stuck here till the day we die. Soon we'll be begging at the door of the mosque on Fridays." She looked down at her tattered slippers. She was sliding her feet into them to get up, so she didn't see his hand reach out—only felt it when it hit her face and knocked her to the side, the air suddenly out of her lungs. She jumped up to get away, but he kicked her so hard that his shoe flew over her head. She landed on her knees, her chin hitting the floor, her teeth shaking in her mouth. She threw his shoe back at him, pushed herself up on her hands, and ran out of his reach, locking herself up in the tiny water closet, as she usually did when they fought. She saw her face in the mirror. Maati's hand hadn't quite landed on her cheek, but there were clear imprints on the side of her neck and jaw. She gripped the side of the sink and let out a long, rasping cry.

She was still in the bathroom when Maati stormed out, slamming the door behind him. She waited for a while to make sure he was gone before coming out and getting a turtleneck to wear under her dress. Maati had already been giving her less and less for running the household. She spent her afternoons in her courtyard, bent on her marma, working on fancy scarves for socialites or bed sheets for brides. Now that Maati had lost his job she knew he'd turn to her for beer money. She let her head drop onto her knees. How did it get to this? Where was the man she'd married? He had been full of promise and energy and ambition, but now he was lazy and angry, ranting at the taxes that cut through his profits, at the customers who didn't leave him tips, at the other drivers for not covering for him when he slipped out to drink.

She wiped her face with her hands, feeling for the welts that were already forming. Lifting her housedress, she looked for the scar from the last beating, when Maati had cut her calf with his belt buckle. Now that the cut had healed, it had the shape of lips, as though he had merely kissed her leg and left a mark. She scratched the skin around it and pulled her sock up.

HALIMA WAITED FOR the bus that would take her to the judge's house in Anfa, a posh seaside neighborhood in Casablanca. Taking a new route made her anxious, and she stood rigidly at the stop, occasionally leaning forward to see if she could catch a glimpse of the bus making the turn onto Place Mohammed V. She wore a light green jellaba and her hair, cut short a few weeks earlier, fluttered in the breeze. She held on tightly to her purse. She'd never had that much money on her. Before leaving her mother's house she had counted the money her brothers had sent when she'd told them she had started her divorce proceedings. She'd snapped each bill between her thumb and forefinger and put them in the envelope that was now tucked in the inner compartment of her handbag.

The smell of rubber and exhaust permeated the air. Near the bus stop a group of day workers squatted, cigarettes between their yellowed fingers, chatting under a cloud of blue smoke. A barber had just rolled up his metal curtain, and now he splashed water on the sidewalk in front of his shop in a futile attempt to get rid of the dust.

Finally an old bus, its front bumper hanging loose, roared up in a billowing cloud of black smoke.

Halima climbed on. The ride would be nearly an hour long, with many stops along the way, but she sat with her back straight, ready to get up at the slightest sign of trouble. A song was playing on the radio, its melody competing with the static from the loudspeakers. She recognized the lyrics to "Fakarouni," by Oum Kalsoum. She willed herself to tune out the music.

The bus stopped near a hospital and a motley group of passengers, beggars, and vendors came on. The last to board was a thin, wiry-haired man who walked slowly down the aisle, holding the handles of each seat as he advanced to the center of the bus. He lifted his shirt, revealing a square pouch taped to his abdomen. The liquid inside looked like urine. He turned around to let everyone have a look. Several people gasped. The man raised a finger upward and recited his complaint in a clear, loud voice.

"Sons of Adam," he said, "this is what God has written for me." He opened the belt that held the pouch in place and showed the healing hole in his stomach. "See what I have to endure every day and thank your God and mine that you don't have to suffer as I do." Nods and clicks of the tongue acknowledged his declaration. "Whoever can help me pay for my hospital bills, may God provide for him, may God open the gates of heaven to him, may God bless him with children, may God protect him from the evil eye . . ." and on he continued with his litany of prayers. Soon hands sprang up, some with coins, some with bills, and the man stopped praying and walked around to collect the offerings.

When he passed Halima's seat he held out his empty palm to her. It had flecks of red paint on it, stuck there from when he'd grabbed the peeling handles of the seats. Looking away from him, she said, "God help us all." The man moved on to willing donors, leaving a trail of hospital smell behind him.

The bus was getting closer to Anfa. Halima held her purse even closer to her side and kept watching for her stop. She stood up as soon as she saw it and got out. Her feet had swelled from the heat, and her blue plastic sandals made creaky noises with every step that brought her closer to the house.

Eventually she found the villa. It was a white stucco building with red Mediterranean tile outlining the roof and windows. It had a well-groomed lawn, a lacquered wood gate, and a fancy doorbell, which Halima rang. A maid, barely a teenager, came to answer. Halima told her she was there to see the judge. The maid gave her a knowing look and told her to wait in the yard. Halima preferred to stay outside. She didn't know whether the judge was married, whether his wife was at home. She wanted to avoid even the appearance of impropriety. So she sat on the doorstep and waited.

The judge appeared at the door. His face was puffy, but his small eyes commanded attention. He peeked out at the street as if he was looking for someone else, then said, "Come inside the yard, don't stand there." Halima was too intimidated to say no. She followed the judge, who waddled inside, his crisp, white jellaba tight around his flabby chest.

"Did you bring the money?" he asked. Halima nodded. With trembling hands, she opened her purse and handed him the envelope. The judge took out the stack of bills and started counting them. He looked inside the envelope again before giving it back to her, then slipped the bills inside the pocket of his seroual. "Next time, don't bring small bills."

Halima swallowed hard. She didn't like his reference to next time. The judge readjusted his jellaba and told her not to worry. "Be on time at the hearing. You'll get your divorce this week." He tapped her back and she realized it was over and he was pushing her toward the door. Suddenly she wished the exchange of money had taken a little longer. Tarik and Abdelkrim had worked so hard to save it and she had waited so long for it and now it was gone. She stumbled and held on to the gate but didn't step out. What if he didn't give her custody? she wondered. She turned around. Why did she give him the money all at once? She could have given him half and promised him the rest after he'd granted her the divorce and custody. Why didn't she think of that earlier? "Wait," she said.

The judge's face, which moments earlier had looked mild if not benevolent, now was menacing. "What?"

"The children," she said.

He frowned. He seemed on the verge of saying something, then decided against it.

"How do I know you're going to keep your word?" Halima's heart beat so fast in her chest that it seemed to her she could hear it in her ears, on her temples, in her hands. "Give me back my money."

The judge looked offended. "I know your type," he said. He put his palm on her back and pressed her toward the door. She stiffened. He withdrew his hand and looked at her with those small, challenging eyes. "Go, before I change my mind."

Halima felt her knees tremble. A knot had formed in her throat, and she tried to swallow it. Why wouldn't he give her the children? This judge had been taking bribes for years; there was no reason to think he wouldn't come through this time. But what if he didn't? How could she trust him? She couldn't trust him, just as she couldn't trust her mother or the sorceress. "Give me back my money," she said, her voice trembling. The judge's eyes opened wide and his lips parted in an expression that was halfway between anger and disgust. He slipped his hand in his pocket and threw the money at her. As the billfold fell to the ground, a few bank notes separated from the rest and floated down. Halima dropped to her knees and clutched them with both hands. The judge grabbed the back of her jellaba and pushed her. She drove her elbow into his gut with all the force she could gather. He bent over in pain, his arms folded over his stomach while Halima stepped outside, a fistful of bills in her hands. The gate slammed shut. Behind her, the yard was already quiet; the judge had gone back inside. She put the money away in her purse and rubbed her bottom with her hand. A Mercedes came noisily down the deserted street, its horn blaring, and the driver turned to look at her, a grin on his face. She ignored him and started walking.

• • •

A FEW DAYS LATER Halima took the bus down-
town to her janitorial job, where she cleaned the offices of
Hanan Benamar, a translator who specialized in immigration documents. Halima had gotten the job through the
center where she'd taken literacy classes, and where a big
banner, which she was able to read at the end of the year-
long program, proclaimed in red block letters: Work for
Your Future—Today. So far, the only use she had gotten
out of the classes was that she could now read the rolling
credits at the end of the soap operas she watched every
night.

Halima knocked on the door twice before inserting her
key and letting herself in. She pushed the gauze curtains
to the side and opened the French windows, letting in the
fresh air. She took in the view of the city, which was dom-
inated by the King Hassan mosque, the three gilded balls
of its minaret shining in the morning sun. Halima began
emptying the trash cans. She was mopping the mosaic
floors dry when Hanan came in. "Sabah el-khir," she said.
She dropped her briefcase on one chair and her jacket on
another.

"Sabah el-khir," Halima said, forcing herself to be
cheerful as she said hello.

Hanan wore a dark pin-striped skirt and a white button-down shirt. Her hair was blown straight, her eyelids darkened with gray eye shadow, her lips a flattering red. I could have been her, Halima thought, as she did almost every time she was in Hanan's presence. I could have been her, had my luck been different, had I gone to a real school, had I married someone else. She wondered now whether Hanan thought the same thing of her and had given her the job only out of pity.

Hanan shuffled through her papers while Halima went about her work. When she finished cleaning up the receiving room, she put the mops in the kitchen cabinet and washed her hands. "I'm done," she announced, and put her jellaba on to leave. Hanan didn't hear, busy as she was staring at her papers.

"Lots of work?" Halima asked.

"Me? Oh, yes," Hanan said. "As long as people want to emigrate, there'll be plenty for me to do."

Without realizing it, Halima slid into the chair opposite Hanan. She thought about her brothers, Tarik leaving one morning when she was still a young girl and Abdelkrim following him only months later, and how there had been no word from either of them for a year. Then the money had started coming, sporadically at first, and later with addicting regularity, and while her mother managed on the payments, Halima, who didn't benefit from their largesse with the same consistency, still lived in the same cement house with the corrugated tin roof and brown water streaming down the middle of the street. She wondered now what would have happened had she, too, gone to Europe like her brothers. Would she have an apartment, a washing machine, maybe even a car? Would she have Maati?

She sat still, and Hanan looked up, a question in her eyes. Halima folded her hands and looked at her shoes. "I was thinking . . ." She wet her lips with her tongue. "How difficult would it be to emigrate?"

Hanan's shoulders dropped. She grabbed a pencil and began tapping it nervously between her fingers. "I'm not a lawyer. I translate documents."

Halima shrugged. "Still," she said. "You'd know."

"Have you seen the lines at the embassies?" Hanan asked.

Halima nodded, even though she hadn't seen them. Maati had told her about them, though, about people queuing up for an entire night just to get a spot inside the buildings, never mind an actual application. He liked taking customers to the embassies because cab fares were higher in the evening, when the lines formed. "But I have my brothers in France," she said.

"Ah," Hanan said. She looked away, as though she was

too embarrassed to say anything, and then drew her breath. "Still, they don't give visas to . . ."

Halima knew what Hanan meant, knew that people like her, with no skills and three children, didn't get visas.

"Take the bastard to court," Hanan said with a sigh.

"I already have."

Hanan blinked, sat back in her chair, at a loss for what to say. The room was quiet, the only sound that of the pencil, still tapping between Hanan's fingers.

"But isn't there some way to get a visa?" Halima asked.

Hanan shrugged. "You have to have a full-time job, a bank account, a ticket, a place to stay—it's complicated," she said, as though Halima couldn't understand anything that required more than three easy steps, like wash, lather, and rinse. I know so much more than that, Halima wanted to tell her. She suddenly felt sorry for having said anything at all to Hanan. It was a mistake to have thought that Hanan or that judge or that magic powder could get her out of her situation.

"There must be some other way," Halima said.

"You mean, go illegally?"

Halima shrugged. She knew what she would say the next time her mother rehashed that old song about being patient: She had to do something for her future—today.

Acceptance

AZIZ AMMOR HAD SPENT the week saying good-bye. So far, he'd visited two sets of aunts and uncles, four friends, and several neighbors, but none of them offered him good wishes for his trip. When they'd found out about his plan to try his luck on a patera, they'd tried to disguise their shocked looks, tapped his back to offer encouragement, and shaken their heads in commiseration. He was getting tired of the silence that his announcement provoked, so he was relieved when, upon hearing the news, his friend Lahcen knocked the table over as he stood up.

"Have you lost your mind, Ammor?" he said. Even though Lahcen and Aziz had known each other since elementary school, Lahcen still called Aziz by his last name, the way schoolboys often did. Aziz and Lahcen had been friends for nearly twenty years now. Together they had snuck into movie theaters, shared their first cigarette, split their first bottle of beer—a Heineken left behind on the beach by a group of preppy teenagers celebrating a graduation. They had also picked up girls together, although it was usually Aziz who did the picking up. Lahcen, Aziz had noticed, never seemed to have much luck with women.

Aziz set the table back on its legs, stealing a glance at his wife, Zohra, who sat on the divan opposite him. She had tried many times to dissuade Aziz, and she watched the scene with the detachment of someone who'd already heard all the arguments, yet who was still curious to see whether they would be resolved any differently this time. Aziz and Zohra had dropped in on Lahcen shortly after the 'asr prayer on Sunday. Lahcen lived with his parents and four sisters in a two-story house in Derb Talian, in the old medina of Casablanca. The window was closed, but the occasional sound of car horns and bicycle bells could still be heard through the glass panes.

"Calm down," Aziz said.

Lahcen opened up his palms and raised his voice. "How can you tell me to calm down? You could drown!" He was like that—he always thought of the worst right away.

"I'm a good swimmer," Aziz said. "And anyway, these days they have motor boats. They'll drop me off on the beach."

"And you think Spain's going to be great? It's all just hard work and ghurba and loneliness."

"At least he'll make a living," Zohra said. Aziz was surprised to hear her jump in with the very words he'd used to persuade her a few weeks earlier. Her family had never liked him—they had let Zohra marry him only because she had been going out with him for three years and the gossip from the neighbors about their "loose daughter" had finished them off. But the marriage didn't help Aziz's tense relations with his in-laws. They had been nagging Zohra about his joblessness, and their comments had grown more persistent after she'd managed to find a job at a soda factory.

When the idea came to him, Zohra had tried to dissuade him, but she gave in after another few months of his unemployment. She said she'd wait for him and when he came back they could move out of his parents' house, have a place of their own, and start a family. In short, she said, they could start living.

"And what about you?" Lahcen said, pointing at Zohra. "He's going to leave you behind?"

"I'll be back in two or three years," Aziz said.

"Haven't we all heard this before?" said Lahcen, his finger on his cheek in a gesture that made him look like a woman. "No one comes back."

"*I* am coming back," Aziz said, his thumb on his chest.

"He will," Zohra said. She took her handkerchief from the sleeve of her jellaba and blew her nose in it. Aziz felt his guilt at leaving her behind pick at him again, and he put his hand on her knee and squeezed it gently.

"Why are you so against this?" Aziz asked Lahcen. "What do you want me to do?"

Lahcen's sister Hakima came into the room, carrying a tray of tea and cookies. Lahcen reached for his pack of cigarettes and walked out. Aziz looked back and forth at the two women, his wife and his best friend's sister, and feeling a little awkward about being left alone with them, got up and followed Lahcen outside.

"So, what do you want me to do?" Aziz asked, as he sat down next to his friend on the steps. He was genuinely curious what the answer would be.

"Try something else," Lahcen said, as he lit his cigarette.

"Like what?"

Lahcen shrugged. "Look at me. I get by." He had invested four hundred dirhams in a few phone cards, and he resold individual minutes at a higher price to people who wanted to make calls at pay phones. He worked out of the central post office in downtown Casablanca. His net gain was tiny, but it paid for his bus fares and his cigarettes. Besides, he declared that he liked it this way, that he always charmed people into buying from him, so he didn't mind the competition from the other phone-card sellers, whether men, women, or children.

"It's different for you. You're single."

"Then why did you get married?"

"What?"

Lahcen pulled on his cigarette. "If you hadn't married, you wouldn't have to do this."

Aziz clicked his tongue. "Leave my wife out of this."

"I'm just saying."

"What do you want me to do? Sell minutes like you?"

"At least I'm doing something. And I don't even have a diploma, like you." The diploma in question was a piece of paper that lay in a folder by Aziz's bed, gathering dust. Both Lahcen and Aziz had flunked their high school exams a few years back, and so they'd been unable to get into a university. Lahcen had started his phone-card operation, but Aziz had gone to trade school, and after two years he was given a degree in automation—which basically meant he could work as a repairman. He hadn't found work.

"Diploma or no diploma, makes no difference."

"You talk like that because you have one."

Aziz sighed. "What is it with you today?"

"I should be asking you that, my friend. You come to me, telling me you're going to get on a boat, risk your life to go to Spain, where you're probably going to get caught anyway, and you want me to congratulate you?"

This version of Aziz's future was one he'd heard before from his parents. They'd warned against the best (a farm job for slave wages!), the worst (a horrible death!), and everything in between (a life of inescapable delinquency!). But he had weighed their warnings against the prospect of years of idleness, years of asking them for money to ride the bus, years of looking down at his shoes or changing the subject whenever someone asked what he did for a living, and the wager seemed, in the end, worthwhile. "Do you have an extra cigarette?" he asked.

Lahcen handed over his pack of Olympique Rouge. "Look, maybe I can help you."

Aziz lit his cigarette and took a long pull. The creaking sound of the door being opened behind them made them turn around. Hakima poked her head out and asked if they were coming in for dinner. Lahcen waved at her and said they'd be in soon. "Go get some bread," Hakima said. "We're out."

Lahcen and Aziz got up and walked to the store, dragging their feet. It was cloudy outside and the wind had picked up. They crossed an empty lot where children played football under a rising cloud of red dust. The piceri had sold most of its bread for the day and had only a few loaves left. Lahcen carefully selected the best-looking one and handed a bill to the cashier, who looked back and forth at the two men, gave them a nasty look, but took the money nonetheless.

"What's his problem?" Aziz asked when they left.

"He's a strange fellow," Lahcen said. "He doesn't like people from outside the neighborhood."

"Ya, what a donkey," Aziz said. This shopkeeper reminded Aziz of his grandmother, who always seemed to find fault with people she barely knew. She found the mailman, a 'arobi from the countryside near Casablanca, to be uncultured and uncouth. To the tailor, a Shamali from the north, she granted slightly higher status, but she often commented that he was too crafty to be up to any good. The Chleuh who sold her mint at the market was often the subject of her invectives about avarice. It had gotten to the point that Aziz had started to have some affection for the very people his grandmother would have disapproved of. Aziz told this story to Lahcen, adding a joke or two to cheer his friend as they headed back to the house for dinner.

"He's nosy," Zohra said, frowning. They were walking back home to the medina. Around them, shopkeepers were locking up for the day.

"He's just concerned," Aziz said.

"So is everyone else."

Aziz didn't answer. He was thinking about what Lahcen had said.

"Do you think he can really do something?" Zohra asked.

Her question was exactly what he feared—that Lahcen's assurances of help would give Zohra hope, a hope that he knew would eat away at her determination to let him go, a hope he knew would eventually be crushed anyway. He held her hand and gave it a squeeze. "If Lahcen could help," he said, "he'd have helped himself."

"You never know," she said.

The next day Lahcen showed up in a blue double-breasted suit, which he'd purchased from the swap meet at Derb Ghallef, where secondhand American clothes were sold, and which he wore on special occasions. "Where are you headed?" Aziz asked, as he greeted him at the door.

"To a meeting," Lahcen said. "And you're coming with me, Ammor." He closed the door behind him.

Aziz knew that he would have to go along with whatever plan Lahcen had hatched, if only for the sake of his parents, who accused him of not having tried every possible solution before deciding to emigrate. "Fine."

Lahcen sat down to have tea with Aziz's parents. He talked about the weather, commented on the latest soccer match, and inquired after their health. Aziz's father responded with a prompt "Hamdullah," teasing his false teeth with his finger, taking them off and readjusting them, while Aziz's mother, a notorious hypochondriac, complained at length about her latest bout of indigestion. Lahcen politely listened, finished his tea, then signaled to Aziz that it was time to go. "Bring your folder," he ordered.

Zohra ran to the bedroom to get Aziz's father's jacket and insisted that Aziz wear it. "For the meeting," she said.

Aziz put it on and stepped outside to meet his friend. "Where are we going?"

"One of the women who buys minutes from me works for a dentist, and I asked her to talk to her boss about you."

"What would a dentist want with me?"

"His chair is broken. Maybe you could fix it, and then he can tell his friends about you."

"That's not a job."

"Let me look at your teeth."

"What?"

"You need to be presentable when you walk into his office."

Aziz laughed. "You know," he said, "I appreciate that you're trying to help me. But this isn't a job, man. It's a one-time thing, isn't it?"

"It might lead to something."

They took the bus downtown and walked into the dentist's office just as a patient was leaving, yelling that she'd never come back. Lahcen held the door open for the woman, letting her finish her diatribe against doctors in general and dentists in particular, then walked in with Aziz behind him. He smiled at the receptionist, asking her how her boyfriend was, the one she always called from the pay phone. "He's fine," she said, her cheeks turning a light pink. "Have a seat, I'll let the doctor know you're here." She disappeared, and Aziz and Lahcen sat down in front of a coffee table upon which lay three half-torn magazines, all of them about golf. Aziz picked one up and started to read while Lahcen crossed his legs and patted his pocket for his cigarettes without taking them out.

The afternoon wore on, punctuated by the sound of the doorbell, the moans of pain, and the *ka-ching* of the cash register. When the clock chimed six, Aziz suggested they leave. Lahcen patted his back and said now that they'd waited this long, they could wait a little longer. Finally the last patient left and the dentist stepped out, taking off his lab coat. He looked at the two men with a mix of surprise and recognition in his eyes. "You're here," he said.

Lahcen and Aziz stood up. The dentist went to the second examination room and pointed to a chair whose headrest was still in its original plastic cover. "I couldn't get it to work," he said, "and the installation company won't return my calls."

While Lahcen chatted with the doctor, Aziz examined the chair. The power cord was plugged in, but when he knelt down to look at the base he saw that there were two additional buttons. He pressed one and the chair made a whizzing sound. "The power wasn't on," he said.

"Oh," said the dentist. Incredulous, he sat down on the stool and pressed various controls with his foot, the chair moving up and down on command. "Well, thanks," he said, standing up, his eyes shifting.

Aziz watched as Lahcen went into a brief but charming speech about how his friend here could fix anything, and if the dentist would tell his colleagues, it would be most appreciated. The dentist nodded vaguely and called out to his receptionist that she could start closing the office. He took out a ten-dirham bill, which he gave to Aziz.

When they stepped out of the office, Aziz took Lahcen's hand and stuffed the bill in it. "For your next pack of cigarettes."

"What's wrong?" Lahcen said.

"What am I going to do with ten dirhams?"

"At least it was something."

"It was a waste of time," Aziz said, pressing the call button for the elevator.

"Don't talk that way. He's going to tell his friends."

"And admit how stupid he is?" Aziz gave up waiting for the elevator and ran down the stairs instead.

"Wait," Lahcen yelled, his voice echoing in the dark staircase.

Aziz heard Lahcen miss a step, so he pushed the button for the timed light and waited for him.

AZIZ WAS CROSSING items off a packing list he'd drawn up. He wanted to take as little as possible, and he was trying to decide whether he should burden himself with a winter coat or not. Zohra suggested he take his waterproof jacket, even though it was a little too small, because it was lightweight and he could fit it into a pocket if he needed to. She had always been the practical one. Even during their courtship, Aziz had felt he was the more romantic of the two, and he'd often wondered if that meant he loved her more than she did him or if she loved him just as much, but in her own, sensible way.

The doorbell rang. It was Lahcen, asking if Aziz would like to go get a cup of coffee. "Sure," Aziz said. There was still plenty of time to worry about packing. They walked to a café just outside the medina, on Place Mohammed V. When the waiter came by with their coffees, Lahcen insisted on paying.

"Still intent on going?" he asked.

Aziz nodded.

Lahcen launched into another speech about why this was a foolish enterprise, but Aziz tuned out after a few minutes. He watched two men, seated across from each other at a table on the street-side terrace, intently leaning toward one another, immersed in their conversation. Whatever they were talking about must have been riveting, because they were oblivious to the pretty college girls passing right by their table. One of the men smiled and touched the inside of the other's arm, rubbing it with his thumb. Aziz looked around him to see if anyone else had noticed the gay couple, but no one seemed to pay any attention.

"Are you listening?" Lahcen asked.

Aziz looked into his friend's brown eyes, and the memories suddenly came back to him of all the times back in high school when Lahcen had put his arm playfully around Aziz's shoulders as they walked back home, or how he found fault with nearly every girl Aziz tried to chat up. When they'd go to the beach, Lahcen would say he didn't want to play soccer, preferring to just lie on the sand. Tapping his hand on the towel next to him, he'd tell Aziz that he needed to learn to relax and enjoy the sun.

"Yes," Aziz said. "I'm listening."

"There was an article in *L'Opinion* about it, man. With photos of the people who drowned and everything."

Aziz nodded. "I know all this."

"And you're not afraid?"

"I just think it will work out."

"You're insane, Ammor," Lahcen said, shaking his head. "And where are you going to get the money?"

"My father," Aziz said. This was not entirely true. Aziz had put together the sum he needed by combining savings from Zohra's meager salary at the factory, a loan from a cousin, and some money from a settlement his father had received when he was in a car accident two years earlier, but he feared that sharing this information would lead to even more entreaties to give it up for the sake of everyone involved.

"Oh," Lahcen said. He drummed his fingers on the table and pushed his coffee cup away.

Aziz felt a twinge of guilt at always dismissing his friend's arguments and turning down his offers of help. "Don't worry about me," he said. "I'm the one who should be worrying about you."

Lahcen looked up, surprised. "Me? Why?"

"Well . . . ," Aziz said, suddenly at a loss for words. A long minute of silence went by, and then he shrugged.

A FEW DAYS LATER, Aziz dropped by the central post office to see Lahcen. He found him standing next to a pay phone, waiting for a customer—a policeman in his gray uniform and white epaulets—to finish his long-distance call. "Have a seat," Lahcen said, as though this public place, where people came and went, was his private office. Aziz sat in the waiting area, watching as a woman in a brown suit argued pointlessly with a teller about unauthorized charges on her phone bill, then left without getting a refund. An old man who cashed a check was immediately surrounded by a band of street urchins asking for change.

"How are you?" Lahcen asked, as he dropped into the plastic chair next to Aziz.

"Fine," Aziz said. "Here, take this." He handed Lahcen the tae kwon do club card he had brought for him.

"What's this for?"

"My sisters bought me a membership as a present three months ago," Aziz said. "And I won't be using it anymore, so I thought you might like it."

"Tae kwon do?" Lahcen said, laughing. "I've never tried it."

"I thought you might like it," Aziz said again, as though sheer repetition could make something come true. "And you might make new friends."

Lahcen turned the card around in his hand and slipped it into his pocket, nodding as if he wanted to humor Aziz. "Now, do you want to go for a cup of coffee?"

"I also brought you these," Aziz said, taking a few of his long-sleeved shirts out of a black plastic bag. He thought that they would be better for Lahcen than those tank tops he always wore to show off his biceps.

Lahcen held one of the shirts up against his chest. "You want me to look like you," he observed.

"I just thought I'd help," Aziz said.

"They probably won't fit."

"Just take them."

"No, I can already see they won't fit," Lahcen said, folding up the shirts and placing them back in the bag. "You keep them." He stood up, an eyebrow raised questioningly, waiting to see whether his friend would follow him.

"Why are you so stubborn?" Aziz asked.

"That's a good one."

Aziz sighed and stood up. "Fine, let's go get coffee."

Lahcen wanted to go back to the same café they'd been to before, near the medina, but Aziz insisted that they go to Ain Sebaa instead. "Why? The place is deserted," Lahcen complained. Aziz replied that he wanted to meet Zohra after she got off work at the soda factory, omitting the fact that he'd convinced her to bring a friend of hers along to the café; he wanted it to be a surprise.

This time Aziz insisted on paying for the coffees. It was sunny, so they sat outside. There were few passersby, but there was quite a bit of traffic, and so they passed the time smoking and staring at the line of French and German cars waiting for the light, the drivers talking on their mobile phones while their stereos blasted American music. Aziz imagined that maybe one day he would be like them, have a car and a place to go to, instead of sitting idle at a coffee shop while his wife was at work.

Soon Aziz saw Zohra walking up the street, arm in arm with her friend, a tall, thin woman in a yellow jellaba that made her skin look darker, the color of toasted almonds. She had long, brown hair, and eyes that sparkled with insouciance. They pulled out chairs for the women, and Zohra introduced her friend as Malika. Zohra's gray-brown eyes looked beautiful under the afternoon light, but Aziz forced himself to pay attention to Malika, to the matter at hand. "So, you work with Zohra," he said.

"Yes," Malika said. She smiled, revealing a gap between her front teeth.

"How do you like it there?" Aziz asked.

"It's okay, I guess," she said, turning to look at Zohra, as if for confirmation of the uninteresting nature of their occupation.

"She's good," Zohra said. "She can check the rims a lot faster than I can." Their drinks arrived, and again Aziz insisted on paying.

Lahcen still hadn't said a word, and in fact had begun surreptitiously picking his nose. Aziz nudged him to stop it. "Do you live around here?"

"No. I live in Derb Gnawa," Malika said, taking a sip from her orange juice.

"My friend is in Derb Talian, so it's not very far," Aziz said. He turned to look at Lahcen, making it clear that he was waiting for him to say something, but Lahcen stirred the sugar in his second cup of coffee and drank it all in one gulp.

This is hopeless, Aziz thought. Nevertheless, he felt he should try again. "Lahcen was just telling me about a new Egyptian movie playing at the Star Cinema."

Malika looked at Lahcen, as if waiting for him to say something, but instead he took out another cigarette and lit it. Malika finished her juice, twirled her straw between her fingers. There was a long, awkward silence, and then Zohra got up and said that they should be on their way.

"So, what do you think?" Aziz asked.

"About what?"

"About Malika, of course."

Lahcen shrugged.

"I think she's cute," Aziz said. "And . . ." he made a gesture as though he were weighing melons.

Lahcen laughed. He put out his cigarette in the ashtray. "Not my type," he said.

"Well, if you told us your type maybe we could set you up."

"Don't you know?" he asked, his voice suddenly raised. "I don't want to be set up."

"Fine," Aziz said.

They lingered in their chairs, watching the sun set over the horizon, the sky changing into shades made even more colorful by the layers of smog over Casablanca. "What about tae kwon do?" Aziz said. "Are you going to try it?"

"We should leave," Lahcen said, standing up.

"Look, I'm sorry." Aziz took his friend by the arm. "Please sit down."

Lahcen took his seat, reluctantly.

"What are you going to do?" Aziz asked.

Lahcen shrugged. "Nothing."

The waiters had come out to turn the terrace lights on. Slowly, mosquitoes gathered around the bulbs, starting a dance of irresistible attraction.

"What if your parents find out about you?"

"Maybe they already know."

They walked slowly back to the bus stop.

ON THE MORNING of his departure, Aziz woke before the alarm clock rang. Zohra was already awake. She sat on her side of the bed, her arms around her knees. "You're coming back," she said, and he couldn't tell from her tone if it was a question or a statement.

"Insha'llah."

She dropped her head in her hands and suppressed a sob. He took her in his arms and held her until her crying subsided. At that moment, if she had asked him to stay, he might not have had the courage to say no. Once again she was the brave one, drying her face quickly and asking him if he was ready.

As he sat for breakfast with his parents one last time, Aziz tried to memorize every sensation he could—the taste of the wheat bread, the smell of the mint tea brewing, the feel of the divan under him, the sound of his father's beads as he fingered them. He knew that in the months that would follow, he would need each one to help him survive. Still, there was something missing from this mental list, and so he got up and told Zohra he would only be out for a few minutes. He ran up to Lahcen's house to catch him before he left for work. Lahcen opened the door, shirtless and in his pajama pants. "I'm off," Aziz said. He hugged Lahcen, with big, gruff pats on the back the way he knew men were supposed to. And then he let go.

Better Luck Tomorrow

WHEN THE AFTERNOON FERRY let out the tourists in Tangier, the guides swooped down on them. They darted from one passenger to the next, offering tours of the medinas and the museums, the palaces and the bazaars. But Murad Idrissi had a different approach. This was his line: "Interested in Paul Bowles?" And it usually worked, especially with the hippie types. Even though the writer had died a few months ago, he could still take the tourists to the house where he had lived, the cafés he'd gone to, the places where he'd bought his kif. These days, though, the guides outnumbered the tourists and Murad found little work.

He watched carefully as passengers got off the Spanish

ferry before he set his sights on a couple. The woman wore a T-shirt and cargo pants; her companion was in a baseball cap and green shorts. The backpacks they carried gave them a forward-leaning gait, but they walked swiftly on the dock. They seemed to be in their late twenties, which wasn't Murad's preferred age range for that line— it usually worked better with older people. Still, he figured they were British or American and would be familiar with Bowles, and the way things had been lately, he couldn't afford to be picky.

They avoided eye contact when he walked up to them, but he recited his line with a suave smile. "Interested in Paul Bowles?" A fleeting expression of surprise lit their faces, but they stepped aside. Shit. Maybe they weren't American. "¿Hablán español?" Murad asked. No answer. Another guide slipped between Murad and the tourists. "Sprechen Sie Deutsch?" he asked. Murad shot the guy a look that said, I saw them first, get the hell away from them. The couple walked on, so Murad followed. In the mesh pocket of the woman's backpack he saw a book. He craned his neck sideways to read the title: *Backpacking in Morocco.* So he was right, they were probably Anglos.

Years ago, when he was still studying for his bachelor's in English, he would go to the American Language Center on Zankat Ibn Mouaz and sit in the library and read all the books he could get his hands on. He loved reading, loved the feel of the paper under his fingers, the way the words rolled off his tongue, how they made him discover things he didn't know about himself.

Murad caught up to the couple at the entrance of the ferry terminal. He willed his voice to ring with confidence as he said, "My name is Murad. Welcome to Morocco! Would you like to visit Paul Bowles's house?"

"No, thanks," the woman said.

An answer at last. There was hope yet. So they weren't interested in Bowles. Well, Murad didn't care much for him either. "Do you want to see Barbara Hutton's palace?" he asked.

"Who's he talking about?" the man asked. From their accent Murad could tell that they were American, not British, as he'd assumed.

"The Woolworth heiress, Jack," the woman said.

Murad realized he had misjudged them—they weren't interested in 1960s Tangier, and so he had to think of something else. Taking a cue from their backpacks, he tried again. "Want to see the Caves of Hercules, Jack? Very, very scenic."

Jack turned around so abruptly that Murad bumped

into him. "Look, I'm sorry," he said. "We don't need a guide. Thanks anyway."

He was impressed by how easily they navigated their way amid the crowd of port employees, busy pedestrians, and countless guides and vendors. Now they were already at the light, with the bus station and the line of cabs just across the street. Time was running out. He stood next to them, looking them in the eye while they stared straight ahead. "I can give you a tour of the medina," he said. The couple continued ignoring him. "Need a hotel room? I know a place where you can get a good price." Still nothing. In desperation, he whispered, "You want some hashish?" His voice was drowned out by the cars that whizzed by in a cloud of black exhaust.

He wasn't sure they had heard him, but when the light changed, there was a slight hesitation in the woman's step. She turned for the first time to look at Murad. Then Jack grabbed her elbow. "Eileen," he said. She had a broad forehead and a fair complexion, but it was her clear, blue eyes that struck Murad. There was something in them that he recognized—resignation, perhaps.

They were now at the Petits-Taxis station. "I can get you a good price," Murad said, his voice at a higher pitch than he wanted, his tone pleading despite himself. He didn't even have any drugs on him, but if they said yes he could always get a cut from one of the dealers. And if they said yes, he could probably make forty dirhams, give or take, enough to pay for the groceries for a few days. Jack's hands tightened perceptibly on Eileen's elbow as he guided her to a cab and opened the door for her. Murad took a deep breath. It was over.

He turned around and looked toward the dock. He considered going back, but by now all the tourists would be gone. He moved on slowly toward Bab el Bahr, the Sea Gate, kicking at rocks on the road. The sole of his shoe came loose. Letting out a string of curses, he pressed the ball of his foot harder against the ground to hide the loose rubber. When he passed the grand mosque, he heard the muezzin call out for the late-afternoon prayer. There would be no more ferries today.

RELUCTANTLY, MURAD HEADED home to the medina. Every day this week he had come home empty-handed, and today was no different. He wandered through narrow streets for a while until he found himself in front of his apartment building. He walked up the stairs to the top floor with the speed of a man being led to face a firing squad. From the landing he heard the catchy theme song to an Egyptian soap opera. He leaned against the metal door of the apartment and let himself in. The warm, wet smell of ironing tickled his nostrils and he sneezed. His mother looked up from her ironing board, where she was pressing his sister's work shirts. Behind her, the only windows in the living room were open, showing a patch of antennas and satellite dishes under the clear sky. He kissed the back of her hand.

"May God be pleased with you," she said.

He took off the jellaba he wore whenever he dealt with tourists. He was now in his old jeans and white T-shirt. He sat beside her, his palms flat against the worn velvet of the divan covers, and heaved a sigh.

"How was your day?" she asked.

"Business is tired," he answered, looking away.

"You'll have better luck tomorrow."

She said this every day, Murad thought, but his luck didn't seem to be getting better. He let his eyes rest on the TV, where a dark, handsome man was courting a plump girl with too much eye makeup, promising her that he would talk to her parents as soon as he had found a job and saved enough money for the dowry. Murad took off his shoe and inspected the sole. "Do we still have some of that shoe glue?" he asked.

"In the cabinet."

Murad went into the only bedroom in the apartment, where his mother and his sister, Lamya, slept at night. He and his younger brother, Khalid, spent the night on the divans in the living room. It was a stroke of luck that the middle children, the twins Abd-el-Samad and Abd-el-Sattar, had earned a scholarship and had started medical school in Rabat just when the family found this apartment, a few months after Murad's father passed away. There wouldn't have been enough space for two more people here. He got the glue from the cabinet and, without bothering to close the uneven wooden doors, went back to the living room. He started working on the shoe.

"Where is Lamya?"

"At work."

Murad's sister, Lamya, was a receptionist for an import-export firm downtown. Bitterly, he recalled how he'd been turned down from a similar job because they wanted a woman. "Shouldn't she be home already?" he asked. His mother ignored him and continued ironing, her eyes on the TV set. "What about Khalid?" he asked.

"He's at school." Murad's mother dipped her fingers in a bowl of water and dribbled it on a shirt sleeve before applying the hot iron. "Why all these questions?" she asked.

"No reason." He capped the bottle of glue carefully, then slipped the shoe under a leg of the coffee table to let it dry.

His mother finished ironing the work shirts, put them on metal hangers, and took them away. When she returned she sat quietly next to him. "Someone asked for your sister's hand today."

"Who?"

"A colleague of hers from work. He came to talk to your uncle and me."

"My *uncle*?" Murad felt his face flush with anger at the slight.

"Well, yes," his mother said.

"Why didn't you tell me?"

"I'm telling you now."

He slammed his hand on the table and got up. "I'm the man in this family now," he said. His father had passed away three years ago, in a hit-and-run accident. He'd been walking home from the café where he drank tea, told stories, and played chess with his friends every evening, when the driver of a red Renault tried to pass a Fiat, veered off the road, and hit him.

"There will be a proper engagement ceremony and you'll be there. May we celebrate when it's your turn."

Murad wondered how his mother could say this so

nonchalantly when she knew that without a job his turn wasn't going to be anytime soon. "I should have been in the know," he yelled.

"Don't raise your voice at me. Are you paying for the wedding?"

"Just because I don't have a job you think I'm invisible? I'm her older brother. You should have come to me."

Murad sat back down on the divan. His eyes were on the TV, but his mind wandered. Lamya was moving on with her life—she had a job and now she was getting married. The twins were still in medical school, but there was little doubt that they had a bright future ahead of them. Doctors could still find jobs. And what about him? He cursed himself. What was wrong with him? Maybe he shouldn't have bothered going to college to study English, spending his time learning a language and its literature. No one cared about these things. In the beginning, when he had just graduated, he'd combed the paper for ads and written long, assured application letters; but as the months and then the years crawled by, he took anything he could find, temporary or seasonal work. Looking back now, he wondered if he should have worked with the smugglers, bringing in tax-free goods from Ceuta, instead of wasting his time at the university.

• • •

AT DUSK, MURAD headed to the Socco Chico. He took a small detour to avoid walking by the Al-Najat building, where he'd had his only promising interview in the six years since he finished college. It took an extra five minutes and he had to walk through a narrow street where brown water pooled at a broken sewer, but it was better than seeing the employees get off work.

He arrived at the Café La Liberté around seven and ordered a cup of coffee. It was thick and tasted like tar. It did nothing for his mood. Around him, turbaned old men smoked unfiltered cigarettes while bareheaded young ones played cards. The TV on the far wall of the café was showing a football match—Real Madrid was playing Barcelona. Murad watched with interest, so he didn't notice Rahal until the man sat down at the table. Rahal smiled at Murad, a smile that looked reptilian because of his large eyes, set too far apart, and his bald head. Murad nodded but continued watching the match.

Rahal ordered mint tea and then poured it, slowly raising the teapot until foam formed in the glass, then he leaned against the blue-tiled wall. "Have you thought about our conversation last week?" Rahal had been hustling Murad, trying to get him to go on one of those boats to Spain, and Murad had already told him twice that he wasn't interested. The man didn't give up easily.

Murad shook his head. "I don't think it's a good idea."

Rahal played with the sugar cube on his saucer. He turned it around and around between his fingers. "Let me ask you something. How much money did you make this month?"

"It's low season right now. Things will pick up in the summer."

Rahal smiled. "You can't be a guide forever. You'll never make a living on it."

Murad took a sip of his coffee and continued watching the match. "Great kick," he said, pointing at the screen. "Barcelona will win."

Rahal didn't look up at the TV. "In Spain," he said "someone like you would get a job in no time."

"I don't know," Murad said.

"Look, I don't usually talk about this, but I can tell. I can tell right away whether someone's going to make it or not. And you will. You're not like the others."

Murad grinned. Did Rahal think he was going to believe that one?

"Suit yourself," Rahal said. "Go play guide. Maybe in ten years you'll have saved enough to move out of your mother's house."

Murad looked down. In his cup, yellowish foam slowly dissolved in the black coffee. "How much?" he asked.

"Twenty thousand dirhams."

Murad shot to his feet. Rahal grabbed his wrist and motioned to him to sit back down. "If I get caught, I go to jail," Rahal whispered.

Murad huffed at him. How could jail scare Rahal? He'd dealt drugs in the past, and now he smuggled people to Spain because it was more profitable. Fifteen years ago Rahal's boss had been a simple fisherman, but now he owned a fleet of these small boats and he'd hired smugglers like Rahal to work for him.

"What about me?" Murad asked, his thumb pointed at his chest.

"You wouldn't go to jail."

"I don't have twenty thousand."

"What about your family?"

"My father is deceased, may God have mercy on him. My mother doesn't have any money. If it weren't for my uncle and my sister, we'd be out on the street."

"Can't they lend you money?"

"Not that kind of money."

"It's a very good price," Rahal said, "We've never had any problems."

"All I can get is eight thousand," Murad said, even as he wondered how he was going to convince his uncle and his sister to let him borrow the sum.

Rahal chuckled. "This isn't some game. We're taking a lot of risk here." He refilled his glass of tea. "We have Zodiac lifeboats, not like the pateras the others use."

Murad called to mind the sunken fishing boats the Guardia Civil stacked on the Spanish coast, plainly visible from the Moroccan side. They thought it would scare people. It didn't.

"Ten thousand," Murad said.

"La wah, la wah. I can't do it for that little."

"You think ten thousand is little?"

"I don't get all of it. I have to pay for the fuel, don't forget. And then there's the police. I have to grease them." Rahal turned the extra sugar between his fingers. With a swift movement he put it in his pocket. "Let me tell you something. You know Rashid the baker? His brother went on one of our boats about eight months ago. Now he's in Barcelona and he sends his family money every month."

Murad never tired of hearing stories like that. He'd heard the horror stories, too—about the drownings, the arrests, the deportations—but the only ones that were told over and over in the neighborhood were the good stories, about the people who'd made it. Last year Rashid's brother had been just another unemployed youth, a kid who liked to smoke hashish and build weird-looking sculptures with discarded matchboxes, which he then tried to sell off as art. Look at him now. Murad took a deep breath. "Twelve thousand. And that's it," he said at last. "By God, I won't be able to get any more out of them." Even though Murad talked about "them," he knew Lamya wouldn't give him a single rial. For one thing, she now had a wedding coming up; for another, he couldn't imagine asking his little sister for help. But it would be different with his uncle. He would talk to him, man to man, and ask for a loan. Surely the old man wouldn't say no, not after having slighted Murad on the wedding of his sister.

"If you make it twenty thousand, I'll get you a job. Guaranteed. Like Rashid's brother."

Murad sighed. "Fine," he said.

"But listen here. People back out. I don't want to waste my time."

"I'm not the type to back out."

Rahal took a sip. "Good. When the time comes, we'll call you. We'll meet on the beach at Bab al Oued."

"When do we leave?"

"When can you get me the money?"

Murad looked away. "Soon," he said.

• • •

AFTER LEAVING THE Café La Liberté, Murad headed back toward the beach. He found a spot near the Casbah where he could get a view of the Mediterranean. It was getting dark. In the distance, car lights from the Spanish side looked like so many tiny lighthouses, beacons that warned visitors to keep out. He thought about the work visas he'd asked for. For the last several years, the quotas had filled quickly and he'd been turned down. He knew, in his heart, that if only he could get a job, he would make it, he would be successful, like his sister was today, like his younger brothers would be someday. His mother wouldn't dream of discounting his opinion the way she did. And Spain was so close, just across the Straits.

He started walking through the Socco. He saw a few tourists wandering down the market. He couldn't understand these foreigners. They could go to a nice hotel, have a clean bed, go to the beach or the pool, and here they were in the worst part of town, looking around for something exotic. He thought of talking to one or two, asking them if they needed a guide, but his heart wasn't in it anymore.

The smell of grilled meat tempted him, and he stopped at a stall that made kefta and brochettes. While he waited for his order he heard a woman speak in English and he turned around to look. It was the one from earlier in the day. What was her name? Eileen. She held a guidebook open in one hand and pointed ahead of her with the other. "I think it's that way," she said. When she looked up and met his gaze, Murad wondered if she recognized him without his jellaba. She smiled. He saw the ease with which she carried herself, the nonchalance in her demeanor, free from the burden of survival, and he envied her for it.

"Do you know where the Café Central is?" she asked. So he had been right about them after all—they'd come to Tangier looking for the Beats. How easy it would be for him to insert himself into their trip now—he could show them the café where Burroughs smoked kif, or the hotel where he wrote *Naked Lunch*. But he was past all that now; he was already thinking about his new beginning, in a new land. He pointed down the street. "This way," he said. "Across from the Pension Fuentes." Then he turned back to wait for his order.

PART II

After

The Saint

FARID HAD SAVED HER. Some people said it was impossible. They said the boy was only ten years old, that he could barely have saved himself, let alone his mother. They didn't believe Halima when she told them that he'd held out a stick and used it to pull her through the water all the way to the shore. They asked her how he got the stick and she said she didn't know. Crazy woman, they said, fingers tapping temples. You have to forgive her, they said, she's been through so much.

But other people believed her. Halima could have drowned with the others, they said. The captain had forced them out of the boat before they could get ashore. The water was cold, the current was strong, Halima didn't know how to swim. Yet Farid had pulled her to safety somehow. And even though the Spanish police were waiting for them right on the beach, at least they were alive. Besides, the boy had helped his sister, Mouna, and his younger brother, Amin, as well. They had *all* survived. Farid was a saint.

Even Halima's husband, Maati, thought it was a miracle. When he'd found out she'd tried to cross the Strait of Gibraltar, he'd kicked the TV off its stand and smashed what remained of the dishes. He told everyone that if all Halima wanted was a divorce, then why didn't she just pay him, like he'd asked her? He'd have divorced her. And what's five thousand dirhams for a woman whose brothers work in France? They could afford it. But to take his children, to run away like this, to risk her life and theirs, well, those were clearly the actions of a crazy woman. Is it any wonder he beat her? But even a hemqa like Halima had done one thing right, he said. She'd given birth to his son, to Farid, and his little boy had saved her life. She was lucky.

AFTER HALIMA RETURNED to Casablanca, she didn't move back in with her mother, who had never agreed with her decision to leave, and who, Halima feared, would try to convince her to get back together with Maati. Instead she borrowed money again, this time from one of her cousins, and took a room with her three children in Sidi-Moumen, a slum outside the city. She couldn't find a janitorial job like the one she had before she left, so she joined the hordes of day workers at the market, spent her time squatting on the dirt road, waiting for a nod from someone who needed laundry washed or spring cleaning done. The vendors arrived first, their carts piled high with oranges or tomatoes or sweet peas. Then the buyers drifted through, haggled over prices, bought their food. After lunchtime the marketplace emptied slowly, and by the time the afternoon prayer was called she'd get up and go home. Sometimes, when she couldn't get a job, when the sun beat down on her until she thought her head would whistle like a kettle, she grew angry with Farid. Why had he saved her? Why had he saved any of them? There wasn't any point in living when all you could do was survive.

Then one day she managed to get one of the vendors, who'd cleared most of his cart by lunchtime, to give her his leftover ears of corn. She planned to barbecue them for dinner. She was fanning the fire with the rabuz when someone knocked at the door. Maati was standing on her doorstep, his body filling the narrow frame. His shirt was open to his chest, displaying hair that had started to go white. His eyes were bloodshot. Halima turned on her heel, scanned the room, trying to figure out where she could hide in such a small place. But Maati grabbed her wrist and, without moving, swung her back toward him. She bit her lip, steeled herself for the blow. But Maati didn't hit her. Instead, he stuffed a piece of paper in her hand. "If this is all you wanted," he said, "now you have it." And, as if to punctuate his declaration, he spit on her. The phlegm landed on her shirt, but all Halima could see was the divorce paper, with the elegant penmanship and unmistakable signature of the 'aduls at the bottom. He turned around and left.

Halima stood, stunned. The fear that had knotted her stomach at the sight of her now ex-husband subsided, and in its stead she felt the rush of blood to her temples. This feeling of elation was entirely new to her. She had tried everything to get this piece of paper, and when she least expected it, it had been delivered right to her doorstep. What had changed Maati's mind? From her mother, Halima had heard that barely a month after she'd run away, Maati had tried to marry again, but the girl's parents had heard about what happened to Halima and turned him down. Maybe he wanted to erase her from his life and start again with someone else. But then she remembered the long train ride from Tangier back to Casablanca, when Farid had turned to her and said, "I wish Baba had divorced you the first time you asked." She'd chuckled at his comment, ruffled his hair with her hand, and turned to look at the scenery outside. Now she folded the sheet of paper carefully and slipped it inside her purse. Her hands still trembling, she put a kettle on the mijmar and made herself a pot of tea. Farid's wish had been granted. She had her divorce. She sat, her chin resting on her hand, thinking about what it meant. And she remembered the bleeding tree.

When Halima was five years old, her mother had come home from the market, excited about the news she had heard: There was a bleeding tree, a holy tree, in Rabat. She'd packed their lunch and they'd taken the train to the capital, riding in the fourth-class cabin, where farmers sat on wooden benches, chatting over their bags, their crates, and their chickens. It was Halima's first trip to the city, and she was disappointed by the quiet streets, the groomed lawns in front of government buildings. The bleeding tree stood in a sparsely planted lot across from the flower market, a few steps away from the police station. A dozen people were there already, some sitting, some standing. From them, Halima and her mother heard the story of the tree. A developer had planned on tearing it down in order to make room for a high-rise, but when the workers tried to fell it, it started bleeding. The pilgrims showed up soon after, some collecting the blood-red liquid for use in concoctions, others using the site as a prayer area. Work had to be halted. Today, someone said, the city had dispatched a scientist to tell people that there was no miracle.

Halima and her mother maneuvered their way to the front line of the crowd, where they could get a better view of the scientist. He was a young man, little more than a teenager, his hair all fluffed up in an Afro like those American singers on TV. He wore a striped button-down shirt and bell-bottom pants. A pencil was tucked behind his ear. He stood, quietly eating sunflower seeds, until everyone settled down. Then he walked up to the tree, flicked open a Swiss Army knife, and made an incision in the trunk. He discarded the piece of wood and, pointing to the blood-red sap, he said that this was a normal substance made by this particular kind of eucalyptus. He called the tree a fancier name, something that sounded like French or Spanish. The tree had been making sap for a hundred years, maybe more. It was perfectly natural.

There was no miracle. There was nothing to see. Go home, he said. People shifted on their legs, looked around at each other, but remained standing. The scientist shrugged and left. Foolish man, people said. What does he know about miracles? He sullied this holy ground. They pointed to the soft, humid earth, where sunflower-seed shells remained, a testament of his passage through the shrine. Halima's mother ran her crooked fingers along the trunk and took some sap, collecting it in a recycled pill bottle.

After the trip to Rabat, Halima's mother returned to Casablanca, full of hope that her arthritis, which had been flaring up lately, would subside; that her prayers would be answered. Halima's father, who always sat on the corner divan smoking unfiltered cigarettes, shook his head and said she was crazy. For a while, however, Halima's mother did get better. She'd started knitting again, and the sound of her needles working formed a soundtrack to every evening for a month. But soon news came from Rabat that the developer had cut the tree down and started work on the new building. When the arthritis flared up again, Halima's mother said it was because the tree had been torn down.

Halima took a sip of her tea. She shook her head. There had been no miracle for her mother, and maybe there was none for her. Still, even if she were to believe those people who said she'd dreamt up the stick and the rescue, she couldn't bring herself to brush off Maati's change of heart. Only a miracle could make that man give her back her freedom. Sometimes, Halima thought, it was better to surrender to things one didn't understand. Her son Farid had given her back her life. Twice. She had to accept that he was different.

That night, when she and the children went to bed on the mat, she lay on her side, staring at him for hours, reliving his young life in her mind. She wondered if there was some other miracle she'd missed because she wasn't paying attention. There was the time when she was walking with him, hand in hand, on their way to the Lakrie market. A motorist made a sharp turn just as she'd stepped off the sidewalk, and his Honda careened toward her. Farid had pulled her back just in time. She'd stood on the pavement, her legs wobbling under her, one hand resting on Farid's shoulders and one on her chest, as though that could quiet the beating of her heart.

She closed her eyes and turned to lie on her back. This boy of hers was a mardi, a blessed child.

KHADIJA, THE NEIGHBOR, was the first to ask. She came to the house one evening, dragging her son Adnan by the hand, forcing him to sit next to her on the mat. She was quiet while Halima made her a pot of tea, using whatever mint and sugar she had left. Farid sat with them while his brother and sister played a string game, making shapes that resembled beds or boats, passing the string back and forth. Halima served the tea, and after the customary small talk, Khadija fiddled with the ends of her housedress, bit her lip, and asked for the favor. She said her Adnan was about to take his grade school exams, that he needed help, a bit of luck. "He already flunked last year," she said. "If he flunks again this year, they'll expel him. Can you imagine, ya Halima? What will I do with him if he doesn't go to high school?" She slapped her cheek for good measure.

"Why don't you keep him home and make him study?" Halima asked, irritated with Khadija for making such a demand. Everyone knew that Adnan had a habit of skipping school to play football on the street.

"But maybe your son can give him a blessing," Khadija insisted. "Didn't you say that he saved your life? Didn't you say that he saved your children's lives?"

Halima nodded, regretfully. Farid rested his head against her arm, as if to comfort his mother for her mistake. She held her palms open before her. "He is only a little boy," she said. "Besides, if he could accomplish miracles, would we be living this way?"

"Let Farid bless my son," Khadija said. "Let him bring us some luck."

"If Adnan studied, he wouldn't need any luck," Halima muttered. Khadija didn't answer. Instead she gave Halima a wounded look. The silence grew heavy, imposing, yet Khadija didn't make any attempt to leave. At last, Halima nudged Farid. He put out his hand, touched Adnan's head, all the while looking away. His first blessing and already an unwilling saint.

HALIMA WAS WASHING the dishes when Farid came up to her. "Is it true?" he asked.

"What?"

"That I'm a saint?"

"Curse Satan, child," she said, shaking her head. "That woman is crazy." She picked up the tray and rinsed it. "Don't forget to take the trash out."

"So why did you ask me to touch her son?"

"Because that was the only way I could get her to leave. Didn't you see?"

Farid nodded.

"You don't mind, do you?" Halima said, reaching out to smooth her son's hair. "It can't hurt, right?"

Farid shrugged. "No."

"At least, this way, she went home happy."

Farid took the trash and walked quietly out. From the kitchen, Halima heard Amin and Mouna teasing him about the blessing. "Touch my nose," Mouna said, laughing. "I think it's running. It needs a little baraka."

"How about my butt?" said Amin. "Maybe my farts will smell like perfume."

Farid slammed the door, but their laughter didn't stop.

EVEN WITH A saint at home, Halima still had to make a living. Her mother had told her about a janitorial job twice a week at a lawyer's office, but when she went to ask she was told that the position had already been taken. So she started selling beghrir at the market. Every year, when people tasted the beghrir she made for Eid, they would compliment her on how fluffy they turned out. Occasionally she'd make a batch of mille-feuilles to entice students going back home from school. She enjoyed working for herself and was good at sales. Things were working out after all, she thought. Sometimes, on her way home from the market, she'd find Adnan playing on the street and she'd drag him by the car all the way to his house, telling him that he'd received a blessing and he shouldn't waste it on football. Before

long Adnan would run home as soon as Halima turned
the corner of the street, her raffia bag balanced on her
head.

One day in June Halima and her children came home
to find Khadija waiting for them, a qaleb of sugar tucked
under her arm. Her son had somehow passed his exams,
and so she gratefully pressed the qaleb into Halima's
hand. Halima murmured her congratulations and turned
to put her key in the lock. Khadija didn't go away. She
stood so close that Halima could feel the woman's warm
breath against her neck. Halima lowered the raffia bag
and held it against her hip. "Adnan must have worked
hard," she said. Khadija didn't seem to have heard. She
kept staring at Farid, an awed look on her face. Halima
pressed her son's shoulders and guided him and his brothers inside the house before turning back to Khadija.
"Uqbal next year. Insha'llah he'll have the same success."

Halima closed the door and heaved a sigh. "Now she's going to want more," she said. "And she's going to tell others."

Farid was already peeling the blue paper off the cone of
sugar. He broke off three pieces and gave one each to his
brother and sister before putting one in his mouth. He
grinned. "You said it didn't hurt."

• • •

A WEEK LATER, Halima was mixing the dough for beghrir when she heard a knock. Mouna opened the door. Halima's mother, Fatiha, shuffled in, leaning on her cane.

"What are you doing here?" Halima asked, getting up.

"Can't I see my own grandchildren?" Fatiha answered, an indignant look in her eyes. "You never bring them around anymore, so your poor mother has to take the bus all the way here to see them." She took off her jellaba and sat down on the mat.

Halima was afraid of what the unexpected visit might mean. Would her mother try to convince her once again to go back to Maati? Would she ask her to stop selling food at the market and get a proper job? Whatever it was, Halima knew the visit could not mean good tidings. "Go play outside," she told the children.

"Wait," Fatiha said. She rummaged for something in her purse, pulled out a handful of sweets. "I brought some candy for them." Amin and Mouna rushed to get their shares, noisily unwrapping the sweets, comparing colors and flavors.

"Have some, Farid," Fatiha said, stretching her crooked hand open for her grandson.

The boy shook his head. "I don't feel like having candy."

"Well, at least come closer, let me look at you," she pleaded.

"I'm just going to play outside." He grabbed the deflated football and took off, trailed by his siblings.

Fatiha clicked her tongue. "Bad manners," she said.

"Can you never say anything positive?" Halima asked. It was just like her mother, she thought, to find fault with three sweet children like Mouna, Farid, and Amin. Fatiha pursed her lips and stayed quiet for a while, watching as Halima poured some batter onto the stone griddle.

"Have you been to the doctor?" Halima asked.

"What for?"

"For your arthritis."

Fatiha grumbled something about having already gone to enough doctors.

"You should go again. These days, they probably have better medication."

"I don't need medication. I'll be fine," Fatiha said, her voice trembling. "Besides, why should I worry about myself when my own daughter doesn't care enough about me to let me have a little blessing?"

Halima shook her head. Her mother's knack for melodrama was something she'd never get used to. She could never get used to people who wanted others to help them out of their problems instead of relying on themselves. She picked up the first beghrir and set it on the tray, then ladled more dough.

"We all care about you, Mmi," Halima said. "Here, have a taste."

Fatiha rolled up the beghrir and took a bite. "God, this is delicious."

"I'll take you to the doctor myself."

"I don't have the money to go to the doctor's."

"Don't worry. I'll pay," said Halima. She reached out and touched her mother's arm as if to comfort her. Then she turned to watch the beghrir break into bubbles as it cooked. She did not notice the fading afternoon light that lengthened the shadows behind her, framing her body like the arches of a shrine.

The Odalisque

THE TEENAGER WAS Faten's favorite client. He wasn't what you would call a regular, like her Friday-night or first-of-the-month men, those who came to her the way they might stop by a bakery and buy an extra pastry to go with their coffee because they'd just gotten paid. In the five months that she'd known him, there hadn't been a regular pattern to his visits, but whenever she saw his car coming up Calle Lucia, she'd arch her back, cock her hip, and smile. He always got out of the car, too, which is more than you could say for the others, the men who talked to her while they bent over their steering wheels, as if spending more than a minute deciding who they were going to fuck was too much of an imposition on their time. He was different.

His name was Martín. At first she'd assumed it was just a fake name, but someone had called his mobile phone once, right after he'd paid her, and she'd heard a hoarse voice at the other end of the line yelling the name. It sounded like a cop—someone with authority, someone used to giving orders. Later on, she asked Martín who it was and he said it was his father, calling from Barcelona to ask why he was out so late, as if Martín were still a child. Martín explained that he was the youngest of his father's children from two marriages. He shook his head and put his phone away, grumbling that el viejo was losing it.

She did not know Martín's last name. What she did know was that he had recently moved to Madrid to attend Universidad Complutense. He never talked about what he studied, and she didn't ask, for she feared it would bring back memories of her own college life back in Morocco and she didn't want to think of that time in her life, when the world still seemed full of promise and possibility.

In a way, Faten liked never knowing when he'd stop by. It gave her something to look forward to, and if he showed up, it was like a gift, something she could unwrap and hold up to admire. The later it got, the better the surprise. And there was, too, the possibility that if he came up to see her late in the night he could be her last one, so it didn't matter how long she stayed with him. That kept her going on bad nights, when it rained or when the girls bickered. The Spanish girls often fought with the Moroccans or Romanians or Ukrainians, but it was a useless battle. Every week there was a new immigrant girl on the block.

Martín reminded her of a neighbor she'd had a crush on when she was little. At that time she had been sent to live in Agadir with her aunt because her mother couldn't afford to keep her in Rabat, what with her father having left them and the child support the court had ordered him to pay never having materialized. Faten had stayed in the seaside town until she turned fourteen and her breasts grew into a D cup. The single man next door had started coming around on the silliest of excuses, asking to borrow a cup of sugar or a glass of oil. That was when Faten's aunt decided it was time for her to go back to the capital.

Faten had moved in with her mother in the Douar Lhajja slum, the kind of place where couscous pots were used as satellite dishes. She'd stayed there for six years—and in that short time she had managed to graduate high school, go to college, find God, and join the Islamic Student Organization. She'd had the misfortune of making a derogatory comment about King Hassan within earshot of a snitch but had, rather miraculously, escaped arrest, thanks to a friendly tip. So when her imam suggested she leave the country, she had not argued with him. She had done as she was told. Except her imam wasn't there when the Spanish coast guard caught her and the other illegal immigrants, nor was he around when she had to fend for herself in Spain. Now no one could decide for her whether or not she could see Martín.

Tonight had been good. She'd made good money and Martín was her last client. She climbed into his car and pulled down the passenger-side mirror, dabbing her face dry with a Kleenex and reapplying her lipstick. She glanced at him. His light brown hair was falling out prematurely, and his thin lips grew thinner whenever he was emotional. He wore a pair of dark slacks and a loose button-down shirt, where gold arabesque letters danced on a sea of deep red. She asked what he wanted to do.

"Just talk," he said. "Can we?"

"Como que no," she said.

He started the car and drove slowly off Calle Lucia, toward Huertas. Faten let her head rest against the seat and stretched her legs, her feet painful from standing too long in high heels. It had been just as hard to get used to the heels as to the short skirts. Before this, back at home, it was always flats or sneakers, an ankle-length skirt, and a secondhand sweater.

"So, where are you from?" he asked.

"Rabat."

"I thought you were from Casablanca."

"I can be from Casablanca if you want." She laughed, wanting him to know it was just a line, not something she'd actually tell *him* with seriousness. She wanted him to know that she thought he was different.

He turned up a side street and stopped the car. She was quiet, watching the lights from the bars up the street, trying to figure out where they were with respect to Lavapiés, where she lived. She spent a lot of time on the street, yet she didn't know Madrid well at all. Since she'd arrived here, she hadn't seen much — only the streets, her apartment, the hospital, and the stores.

Martín spoke softly. "How long have you been in Madrid?"

"Three years, just about."

"I bet you have a lot of regulars."

"A few. Not a lot."

"They don't know what they're missing."

"And what would that be?"

He circled the knob of her knee with his thumb. "So

much," he said. "I like the smell of your skin—salty like black olives." He coiled a strand of her hair around his finger, let it spring out, ran his fingers along her cheekbones, cupped her right breast. "And your breasts—ripe like mangoes."

"You're making me sound like a dish," she said.

"I guess you could say I'm a connoisseur."

She looked into his eyes, and for the first time she wondered if what she had assumed was a flicker of innocence was something else—a twinkle of playfulness, even mischief. "There's something I've been meaning to ask," she said. "About your father. Is he a cop?"

"He's a pig."

"Why do you call him that?"

"Because he's a fascist," he said. He leaned back against the headrest as he spoke, telling her about his father, a retired army lieutenant who had served under Franco as a young man. It was a bit of a tradition in the family, Martín's grandfather having served under Franco as well. Hearing the Generalissimo's name stirred in Faten memories about her maternal grandfather, a proud Rifi who'd lost his eyesight during the rebellion in the north. It was mustard gas, he'd told his children, and he'd spent the rest of his life begging for a gun to put an end to it all. It was cancer that took him away, though, two years before Faten was born.

Martín said his father hated the immigrants. He shook his head. "But I'm not like him," he said. "I like you."

"You do," she said, in her I've-heard-it-all-before voice.

Martín didn't seem to mind the sarcasm. "I want to help you," he said, stroking her arm. He said he could help her get her immigration papers, that he knew of loopholes in the law, that she could be legal, that she wouldn't need to be on the streets, that she could get a real job, start a new life.

Faten had never expected anyone to make extravagant promises like these, and so she wasn't sure whether she should laugh or say thank you. For a moment she allowed herself to imagine what a normal life would be like here, never having to see the men, being able to sleep at night, being able to look around her without worrying about the police at every turn. She began to wonder about the price of all this—after all, she had long ago learned that nothing was free. He laughed when he noticed her fixed gaze. "But first, tell me about yourself. Where did you live in Rabat?"

She shrugged. "An apartment."

"With your parents?" he asked.

"My mother."

"Any brothers or sisters?"

"No."

"That's unusual, isn't it?" he asked. "I mean, being an only child, in your country."

"I guess."

"And did you wear those embroidered dresses? What are they called? Caftans?"

"Not really."

He seemed disappointed and, looking down at the steering wheel, he bit his fingernails, tearing strands of cuticle with his teeth.

"What's with all the questions?" she asked. "Are you doing a term paper about me?" she joked.

He threw his head back and laughed. "Of course not," he said, slipping his hand down her thigh. She burrowed through her purse, looking for condoms, and discovered she was out. When she told him this, he said he had extras in the glove box. She opened it and, there, between CDs, maps, and gas-station receipts was a copy of the Qur'an.

"What's this?" Faten said, sitting straight up, holding the book in her hand.

"Don't touch that," he said, putting it back.

"Why? Is it yours?"

"Yes, it's mine."

She blinked. The brusque tone was not something she was used to from him. "Why do you have it in your glove box?" she asked.

"I'm just reading up," he said. He reached out and caressed her hair. "Can we get on with it?"

She nodded her head and passed him the condom. In her experience with men, she'd long concluded that even when they said they only wanted to talk, they always wound up wanting some action, too. Maybe Martín was no different after all.

When it was over she adjusted her miniskirt and buttoned her corduroy jacket. Martín's questions and his offer of help had caught her unprepared; his wanting to have sex had disappointed her. She felt the same sadness that she had felt as a child, when she'd discovered that the silkworm she'd raised in a shoe box and lovingly fed mulberry leaves had died, despite all her care. She'd cried all day, wondering what she could have done differently to keep the worm alive, until her aunt came home and told her that that was what happened sometimes with silk worms—they died no matter how carefully you took care of them.

He started the engine. "I'll drop you off if you want."
She opened the door and got out. "I'll just take a taxi."

FATEN CLIMBED THE STAIRS to her apartment just
as the garbage trucks were making their rounds. She heard
one of the men hollering at another in Moroccan Arabic,
telling him, as he emptied a bin, that the family at 565
had just had a baby. Cleaning out people's trash, the men
got to know everything about everyone's lives. Sometimes
Faten felt that way about herself, as though she had been
entrusted with people's secrets and her job was to dispose
of them.

Faten found her roommate, Betoul, in the kitchen eating breakfast. Betoul worked as a nanny for a Spanish
couple in Gran Vía, and she had to take an early bus in
order to get there before 6:30, when the lady of the house
required her help. Sometimes Betoul couldn't resist talking about her bosses, how the wife was given to depres-
sion, how the husband liked to read his newspaper in the
bathroom, leaving urine stains on the floor. But Faten
didn't like to hear about the husband at all. She heard
enough from the men in her job.

Betoul was from Marrakesh, where she had two
younger sisters in university, one brother who worked as

a photographer, and another who was still in high school. She was one of those immigrants with the installment plan—she sent regular checks in the mail to help her brothers and sisters. In addition, she lived like a pauper for eleven months of the year, and then, in August, she flew home and spent whatever was left in her bank account. Of course, her yearly trips only made people back home think that she made a lot of money, and so she always came back with long lists of requests in her hand and new worry lines etched on her forehead.

In Morocco Betoul would never have lived with Faten, but here things were different. Here Betoul couldn't put on any airs, the way she would have at home. She had moved in with Faten because the rent was cheaper than anything else she could find, allowing her to save even more money to send home.

Faten dropped her bag and keys on the counter. "Good morning."

"Morning," Betoul said. "You left the door unlocked last night."

"I did? I'm sorry."

"You should be more careful. Someone could have gotten in here."

"I'm sorry," Faten said. "I've been distracted lately."

Betoul nodded and finished her slice of buttered bread. She drank the rest of her coffee standing. Then she put a few grains of heb rshad in a hermetically sealed plastic bag, which she stuffed in her purse.

"What's that for?" asked Faten.

"For Ana," Betoul said. Ana was the toddler, the youngest of the three children whom Betoul watched while their parents worked. "She's had a bit of a cold, and so I thought of making her some hlib bheb rshad."

"Why do you bother?" Faten asked.

Betoul zipped her purse closed.

"I'm sure Ana's mother wouldn't want you giving that to her anyway," Faten said.

"What would you know of what she wants?"

"She'll probably laugh at you and throw it out."

"You're the one that people laugh at—the way you sell your body."

Faten felt her anger take over her fatigue. She had been wary of having Betoul as a roommate. She'd heard a rumor that back home, when Betoul had found out that her husband, a truck driver, had been cheating on her with a seamstress from Meknès, she'd put a sleeping pill in his soup and then drawn X's on his cheeks with henna while he slept, leaving him marked for days. Faten had finally agreed to room with Betoul because she wanted someone with a day job, someone whom she wouldn't see much.

"I'm not forcing you to stay here," Faten said. "You can move if you want."

Betoul left, slamming the door behind her.

ORDINARILY, AFTER FATEN came home she took a shower, slept until two, and then took a sandwich to the park and watched old couples feeding the pigeons or young ones kissing on the benches. If the weather was too cold, she watched television or went shopping. But today her routine was already off. She couldn't sleep. She stared at the ceiling for a while and then turned to look at her nightstand, where a pocket-size edition of the Qur'an lay, a thin film of dust over it. She remembered her college days, when she'd decided to wear the hijab and preached to every woman she met that she should do the same. How foolish she had been.

She thought about her best friend, Noura, back in Rabat, and wondered what had happened to her, whether she'd kept the hijab or whether, like Faten, she'd taken it off. Noura was probably still wearing it. She was rich; she had the luxury of having faith. But then, Faten thought, Noura also had the luxury of having no faith; she'd probably found the hijab too constraining and ended up taking it off to show off her designer clothes. That was the thing with money. It gave you choices.

She tried to chase Noura out of her mind. That friendship had cost her too much. She knew that Noura's father, who'd taken a dim view of their friendship, had pulled some strings to have her kicked out of the university. If it hadn't been for him, maybe Faten would have graduated, maybe she wouldn't have been so careless in that moment of anger, maybe she wouldn't have said what she did about the king, maybe she would have finished school and found a job, maybe, maybe, maybe.

She got out of bed and went to the bathroom to get a Valium. The main thing to survive this life here was to not think too much. She poured herself a glass of water in the kitchen. Her eye fell on Betoul's calendar, taped to the side of the refrigerator. The Eid holiday was coming up and Betoul had circled the date, probably so she could remember to send a check to her family. It made Faten nostalgic for celebrations, even as she knew there was not much to be nostalgic about. After she had moved back in with her mother in Rabat, Eid amounted to an extra serving at dinner. There were never any new clothes to wear or a barbecued lamb to eat or shiny coins to feel in her pocket.

Still, she had a certain fondness for those special times because at least her mother didn't work on Eid and they could spend the day together. She pushed the memories out of her mind and shuffled over to the living room.

She lay on the sofa, waiting for the Valium to kick in. There was a program on TV about dromedaries, and she watched, eyes half-closed, as the Spanish voice-over described the mammal's common habitat, his resistance to harsh living conditions, his nomadic patterns, and his many uses, as a beast of burden, for his meat and milk, and even for his dung, which could be burned for fuel. Soon Faten's eyelids grew heavy and she fell asleep.

When Martín showed up again a week later, she didn't feel the same sense of glee that she'd had in the months she'd known him. He came out of the car to ask her to join him, and she hesitated. "What's wrong?" he asked.

She shrugged, her eyes scouring the other cars, but he wouldn't leave. "What do you want?" she asked.

"What do you think?" He laughed. She wasn't sure whether it was with her or at her. He held out his hand and she took it and followed him to the car. Again he drove out to Huertas. A song by Cheb Khaled was on the

CD player, and as she listened to the lyrics she wondered whether Martín knew what they meant.

After a few minutes, Martín asked her where she grew up, as he had done the last time, as though he were checking that her answers hadn't changed. This time, she had no illusions about what he wanted. She looked out of the window. "Casablanca," she said.

She thought about her first john, her first week in Spain. The captain of the boat that had brought her here hadn't bothered to land in Tarifa; he'd started turning back as soon as they were within swimming distance of the coast. She'd managed to get to the beach, where the Spanish Guardia Civil was waiting for them. Later, in the holding cell, she saw one of the guards staring at her. She didn't need to speak Spanish to understand that he'd wanted to make her a deal. She remembered what her imam had said back at the underground mosque in Rabat—that extreme times sometimes demanded extreme measures.

The guard had taken her to one of the private exam rooms, away from everyone else. He lifted her skirt and thrust into her with savage abandon. He was still wearing the surgical gloves he'd had on to examine the group of migrants who'd landed that day. And, all the while, he kept calling her Fatma. And he said other words, words she didn't understand, but that she'd grown used to now. Over the years that followed, she'd had time to hear all the fantasies, those that, had she finished her degree, she might have referred to disdainfully as odalisque dreams. Now they were just a part of a repertoire she'd learned by heart and had to put up with if she wanted to make a living.

"Where did you grow up?" Martín asked.

"In a Moorish house."

"With your parents?"

"I didn't see much of my father. I spent all my days in the harem."

"With your siblings?"

"With my six sisters. They initiated me into the art of pleasing men."

Martín chuckled. She could tell he was pleased with the game.

"Why do you come to me?" Faten asked. "There are a lot of girls out there. Like Isabel, and—"

"Women in this country," he said, shaking his head. "They don't know how to treat a man. Not the way you Arab girls do."

Faten felt anger well up in her. She wanted to slap him.

"I've been reading up," he said. "About the duties of

the woman to the man and all that. It's a fascinating subject."

She watched his clear, open face become excited as he told her that he *knew* things about her and her people. That was the trouble with him. For all his studying, all his declarations of understanding, he was no different than his father. He didn't know anything.

She stared at Martín in silence, trying to visualize herself in the way he saw her, the way he wanted her to be—that was the price she would have to pay every time if she wanted to see him. When he started talking about how he would help her get her immigration papers in order, how he cared about her, she raised her palm to stop him. "I don't need your help," she said.

He gave her a look that made her feel he didn't believe her, then continued talking, as though her acquiescence wasn't required when it came to the matter of helping her, because he knew what was better for her.

"Time's up," she said.

He got his wallet out, continuing to explain his plans for her.

"From now on, all the chitchat is extra," she added.

He stopped talking, eyebrows raised in surprise, then handed her a few more bills, which she pocketed.

"I think you should find yourself someone else next time," she said. She opened the car door and got out.

FATEN HADN'T SEEN Betoul for ten days. Her schedule had miraculously adjusted after their sharp exchange, to the point that Faten always seemed to come home only a few minutes after Betoul left. Faten would walk in to find the toaster still warm, the dishes still dripping on the rack. By the weekend, Faten decided to do something. She was going to cook a meal for Eid and so, rather than sleep, she spent the better part of her day at work in the kitchen. At home with her mother, meals had been simple—fava beans and olive oil, rghaif and tea, bread and olives, couscous on Fridays, whatever her mother could afford to buy. Now that Faten could buy anything she wanted, she didn't know how to make the dishes she'd craved as a teenager. The lamb came out too salty and the vegetables a little burned, but she hoped that Betoul wouldn't mind. She rounded off the meal with pastilla from the Moroccan bakery at the corner, set the table, and waited.

When Betoul finally came home, she stood for a moment, with her hand still on the door knob, and exhaled loudly.

"How was your day?" Faten asked.

"I'm exhausted."

"Is Ana still sick?"

"No, she's better," Betoul said. "But her mother spent all day in bed, crying. She didn't go to work. She said she's too fat and her husband doesn't want her anymore. So after I took the children to school and put Ana down for her nap, I made her lunch and then let out the waist on a couple of her pants, so they'd fit better."

"Well, you should rest now. I made dinner," Faten said.

"Aren't you working tonight?"

"Not tonight," Faten said. "It's Eid."

Betoul looked as though she wanted to sleep rather than eat, but she said thanks, went to wash up, then sat at the table. Faten served her a generous portion of the lamb. Betoul had a taste. "A bit salty, dear," she said.

Faten smiled, feeling grateful for the truth.

Homecoming

FOR FIVE YEARS Aziz had imagined the scene of his homecoming. In his carefully rehearsed fantasies, he would come home on a sunny day, dressed in a crisp white shirt and black slacks, his hair gelled back and his mustache trimmed. His new car would be stacked to the roof with gifts for everyone in the family. When he rang the doorbell, his wife and his aging parents would greet him with smiles on their faces. He would take his wife into his arms, lift her, and they would twirl, like in the movies. Within days of his arrival, he would move them from the decrepit apartment in a poor neighborhood of Casablanca to one of those modern buildings that sprang up daily in the city.

But as the date of his return to Morocco approached, Aziz found that he had to alter the details of his daydreams. He had imagined he'd arrive in a late-model car, but now he thought that a car trip would be impractical, and besides, he didn't think his beat-up Volkswagen could sustain the 800 kilometers from Madrid to Casablanca. So he had booked himself on a Royal Air Maroc flight instead. To make matters worse, the image of his family greeting him at the door of their apartment grew dimmer. His father had died during his absence, and now his mother and his wife lived alone. He also had trouble visualizing his wife's face as easily as he had in the beginning. He remembered her to be slender and distinctly shorter than he, but he couldn't quite recall the color of her eyes, whether they were green brown or gray brown.

These uncertainties made for a stressful few days, culminating on the day of his departure. He arrived at Barajas Airport three hours before his flight. He made sure again and again that his passport and work visa were in order so that he could reenter Spain after his trip. Once he got on the plane, he couldn't eat the light meal they served during the hour-long flight. He filled out his customs declaration as soon as it was handed to him, repeatedly checking to see that he had entered the correct information from his passport.

When finally the plane flew over the port of Casablanca, he looked out the window and saw the beaches, the factories, the streets jammed with cars, the minaret of the King Hassan mosque, but he couldn't locate the medina or the dome in the Arab League Park. He held on to the arms of his seat as the plane began its descent.

It was Aziz's first time inside the Mohammed V Airport in Casablanca. He had left the country on an inflatable boat out of Tangier, in pitch dark, with two dozen other immigrants. He had been caught right on the beach in Arzila by the Spanish Guardia Civil and sent back to Morocco on the ferry two days later. He had spent a few months in Tangier, hustling, and tried again to cross, on a balmy summer night. This time the current had helped him, and he had landed on a quiet beach near Tarifa. A few days later he was in Catalonia, ready for the farm job he had been promised by one of the smugglers he'd paid. It was tough work, but at least it was work, and he tried to keep his mind focused on the paycheck at the end. What he remembered most about that first summer was the hunched figures of his fellow workers and the smell of muscle ointment inside the van that they took to work every morning. When the long-awaited paycheck turned out to be a pittance, he was too afraid to complain. He thought of going north and crossing into France but was afraid to tempt fate again. After all, he had already been luckier than most. The trip in the inflatable Zodiac had been an ordeal he wanted to forget, and he didn't think sneaking across the border in the back of a vegetable truck would be any easier. So he traveled south instead. He arrived in Madrid in November, with only a vague address for a friend who worked in a restaurant and might be able to help him out.

THE CASABLANCA AIRPORT was impressive. The marble floors, the automatic doors, the duty-free shops—everything looked modern. But the line for passport check was long. After waiting an hour for his turn, Aziz stood at the window where the officer, a man whose purple lips attested to heavy smoking, cradled his chin, an unfriendly look on his face.

"Passeport," he said.

Aziz slid the green booklet bearing the imprint of the pentacle under the glass window. The officer typed something on his keyboard, then leafed through Aziz's passport.

"Where do you work?" the officer asked.

Aziz was taken aback. "In an office," he said. That was a lie. But he didn't understand what his job had to do with checking his passport. He feared that telling the truth, that he was a bus boy, would make the officer look down on him.

"Do you have your national ID card?"

"No." Aziz stiffened. He stood with his back straight, trying to control the surge of anxiety that was overtaking him. He didn't want to appear nervous. The officer sighed audibly and started typing away again at his computer. He stamped the passport and threw it across the counter. "Next time, have your ID with you."

Aziz walked to the luggage area and collected his bags. The customs officer asked him to open his suitcase, prodding the contents with his baton. He saw a pack of ten undershirts, still in their plastic wrapping. "Are you planning on reselling any of these?" he asked.

Aziz knew the type. They harassed immigrants in the hope that they would get a bill slipped to them. He didn't want to play that game. His voice was cool and disaffected when he replied no. The officer looked behind Aziz at the line, then closed the suitcase and marked it with a check mark in white chalk. Aziz was free to go.

He rode the escalator down to the train station. The shuttle train had been nicknamed Aouita, after the Olympic gold medalist, because it was fast and always on time. Aziz smiled now at the thought of it, at how his countrymen were always quick to come up with funny names for everything. He took a seat on the train, which departed right on time. Outside, the road was littered with black plastic bags. Trees, their leaves dry and yellow, swayed in the wind. In the distance an old truck lay on its side, abandoned, its wheels in the air. Soon they entered the metro area, with its factories and apartment buildings.

He got off the train at Casablanca-Port, the stop nearest to his old neighborhood. As he stepped into the lobby of the station, he found himself in the middle of a crowd of boys selling cigarettes, men offering to polish shoes, beggars asking for change. He held his suitcase and handbag firmly. His throat was dry. He started walking in earnest—the apartment was a short distance from the station and there was no need to take a cab. The cart that sold boiled chickpeas in paper cones was still there up the street, and the same old man in a blue lab coat and wool hat still worked at the newspaper stand. A group of teenage girls on their way to school crossed the street in Aziz's direction. Several of them had scarves on their heads, and despite himself Aziz stared at them until they had passed him.

When he arrived at the marketplace entrance, the vendors were still opening their shops, preparing their displays of fruits, vegetables, and spices. A butcher was busy hanging skinned lambs and cow's feet. Aziz felt nauseous at the sight of the meat. Carts creaked behind him as the drivers rushed to make their deliveries. Shouts of "Balak!" warned him to stand aside, and twice he had to flatten himself against a wall to avoid being run over. He felt beads of sweat collecting on his forehead, and the unbearable weight of his sweater on his chest. He wished he could take it off, but both his hands were busy and he was too nervous to stop before getting home.

Aziz turned onto a narrow alley and continued walking until finally he found himself at the entrance of the building, a rambling, turn-of-the-century riad that had been converted into small apartments. Aziz crossed the inner courtyard and knocked on the door of the apartment. The only response he received was from his own stomach, which growled as it tied a knot. He looked over toward the window and saw that the shutters were open. He knocked again. This time, he heard footsteps rushing and there she was, his wife.

"Ala salamtek!" Zohra cried.

"Llah i-selmek," he replied. She put her arms around him and they hugged. Their embrace was loose at first but grew tighter. Aziz's mother shuffled slowly to the door, and she wrapped one arm around him, the other one holding her cane. She started crying. Aziz let go of both women, grabbed his suitcase and handbag, and stepped inside.

The apartment was darker than he remembered. The paint on the walls was flaking. One of the panes on the French windows was missing, and in its place was a piece of carton; but the divan covers were a shiny blue, and there was a new table in the center of the room.

Aziz's mother broke into a long ululation, her tongue wagging from side to side in her toothless mouth. She wanted all the neighbors to know of the good news. Zohra joined her, her voice at a higher pitch. Aziz closed the door behind him, and now they all stood in the living room, laughing and crying and talking.

Zohra looked thin and small, and she had defined lines on her forehead. Her hair was tied in a ponytail. Her eyes—he saw now that they were gray-brown—were lined with kohl. Her lips had an orange tint to them. She must have rubbed her mouth with roots of swak to make her teeth whiter.

"Are you hungry?" Zohra asked.

"No," Aziz said, his hand on his stomach. "I couldn't eat."

"At least let me make you some tea." Aziz knew he couldn't turn it down, and besides, he longed to taste mint tea again. Zohra disappeared into the kitchen and he sat next to his mother. Her eyes scrutinized him.

"You look thinner," his mother said. She herself seemed to have shrunk, and her shoulders stooped. Of course, he told himself, it's been a few years, it's normal. "And your skin is lighter," she added. Aziz didn't know what to say to this, so he just kept smiling as he held her wrinkled hand in his.

Zohra came back with the tea tray. Aziz sat up. She was still very beautiful, he thought. When she gave him his glass of hot tea, he noticed that her hands seemed to have aged a lot faster than the rest of her, the skin rough and dry. Her knuckles were swollen and red. He felt a twinge of guilt. Perhaps the money he had sent hadn't been enough and she'd had to work harder than he thought to make ends meet. But it hadn't been easy for him, either. He took a sip.

"Let me show you what I brought for you," he said. He put down his glass and went to open the suitcase. He took out the fabric he brought his mother, the dresses for Zohra, the creams, the perfumes. The two women oohed and aahed over everything.

When he took out the portable sewing machine, Zohra looked at it with surprise. "I bought one last year," she said. She pointed to the old Singer that lay in a corner of the room.

"This one is electric," he said proudly. "I'll install it for you. You'll see how much faster it is."

WITHIN AN HOUR of his arrival, a stream of visitors poured in to see Aziz. The tiny apartment was filled with people, and Zohra kept shuttling between the kitchen and the living room to refill the teapot and the plate of halwa.

"Tell us," someone said, "what's Spain like?"

"Who cooks for you?" asked another.

"Do you have a car?" asked a third.

Aziz talked about Madrid and how it could get cold in the winter, the rain licking your windows for days on end. He also talked about the Plaza Neptuno, near the Prado, where he liked to wander on summer days, watching the tourists, the vendors, and the pigeons. He spoke of his job at the restaurant and how his manager liked him enough to move him from dishwashing to busing tables. He described the apartment in Lavapiés, where he lived with two other immigrants. They took turns cooking.

"Did you make friends?" someone asked.

"Some," Aziz said. He mentioned his neighbor, who had always been kind to him, and his boss at the restaurant. But he didn't talk about the time when he was in El Corte Ingles shopping for a jacket and the guard followed him around as if he were a criminal. He didn't describe how, at the grocery store, cashiers greeted customers with hellos and thank yous, but their eyes always gazed past him as though he were invisible, nor did he mention the constant identity checks that the police had performed these last two years.

Zohra's mother, who lived down the street, had also dropped by, and she sat quietly through all the conversations. Finally she asked, "Why would you work there while your wife is here?" She clicked her tongue disapprovingly. Aziz looked at Zohra. He wanted to talk to her about this, but they hadn't had any time to themselves yet. He cleared his throat and refilled his mother-in-law's glass.

"Where is Lahcen?" Aziz asked. "I thought he'd be here by now." He and Lahcen had exchanged letters in the beginning, but as time went by, they had lost touch. Aziz had received the last postcard from Lahcen two years earlier.

"He's moved to Marrakesh," Zohra said. "Everyone has mobile phones now, so he couldn't sell phone cards anymore."

AFTER THE GUESTS left, Aziz's mother went to spend the night with the neighbors next door so that he and Zohra could have the apartment to themselves. Aziz stepped into the bedroom to change into a T-shirt and sweats. He sat at the edge of the bed and looked around. There was a faded picture of him tucked in a corner of the mirror on the old armoire and a framed one, of the two of them on their wedding day, hanging on the wall by the door. Under him, the mattress felt hard. He bobbed on it and the springs responded with a loud creaking.

Zohra busied herself for a while in the kitchen before finally turning off the lights and coming into the bedroom. She had been talkative and excited during the day, but now she seemed quiet, shy, even. Aziz sat back against the pillow and crossed his legs.

"You must be tired," Zohra said, her eyes shifting.

"I'm not sleepy yet," Aziz said.

Zohra looked ahead of her, at the street lights outside.

"I have something to tell you," he said. He swallowed hard. Zohra looked at him intently. "I have some savings. But . . . " He swallowed again. "I don't think it's enough."

Zohra sat on the edge of the bed. "How much?" she asked, a look of apprehension on her face.

"Fifty thousand dirhams," he said. "It could have been more, but the first year was tough."

Zohra reached over and took his hand in hers. "I know it was."

"There was the rent. And the lawyer's fees to get the papers. And the money I had to send every month."

"Fifty thousand is a lot. You could use that for a start. Maybe start a business?"

Aziz shook his head. "It's not enough."

"Why not?"

"That would barely cover the lease for a year. Then there's inventory and maintenance." Aziz shook his head. "Not to mention all the papers." He thought of the lines he had seen in government offices, people waiting to bribe an official to push their paperwork through.

"So what are we going to do?" Zohra said.

"Go back to Spain," Aziz said, looking down. His wife had sacrificed so much already. Her parents had only agreed to let her marry him because they thought that at the age of twenty-four it was better for her to be married to someone who was jobless than to stay single. She had stood by and helped him save for the trip, waited for him, but at least now she wouldn't have to wait any longer. "And I've started your paperwork, so you will be able to join me before long, insha'llah."

Zohra let go of his hand. She nodded. Then she stood up and turned off the light. He heard her take off her housedress and get on the bed, where she lay on her side. When he got closer, she stayed still, her knees to her chest. He moved back to his side of the bed and tried to sleep.

THE NEXT DAY, Aziz was startled out of his slumber at five by the sound of the muezzins all over the city. He lifted his head off the pillow for a few seconds before letting it rest again and, eyes closed, listened to them. In Spain he missed the calls for prayers, which punctuated everything here. He smiled and fell back to sleep. Later the sound of cars and trucks whizzing by the industrial street a few blocks away from the apartment did not wake him. But the smell of the rghaif Zohra was making was too much to ignore, and he finally got out of bed around nine.

When he came out his mother was sitting on the divan in the living room, looking regal and aloof. He kissed the back of her hand, and in response she said, "May God be pleased with you." Zohra entered the living room and, seeing him there, went back to the kitchen to get the tray of food. She placed the communal plate in the middle of the table, pushing it a little closer to Aziz. She poured and passed the tea around. Then she brought a glass of water and a pill for Aziz's mother.

"What's the pill for?" Aziz asked.

"Blood pressure," Zohra said. She sat down and started eating.

"I didn't know." He struggled to think of something else to say. "The rghaif are delicious."

"To your health," she replied.

He chewed in earnest, relieved that, with his mouth full, he couldn't say anything. Fortunately a knock on the door provided some distraction. A little girl came rushing in without waiting to be let in. She looked about six years old. Her hair was in pigtails and her blue pants were ripped at the knees.

"Who is she?" Aziz asked his mother.

"Meriem, the neighbors' kid. She's always here."

The child jumped into Zohra's arms, and Zohra laughed

and planted loud pecks on her cheeks. "Do you want something to eat?" Zohra asked. She sat the child on her lap and handed her a rolled rghifa, dipped in melted butter and honey. She smoothed her hair and tightened her pigtails. Later Zohra took Meriem to the kitchen, and when they emerged the little girl was holding a wooden tray loaded with fresh dough on her head. She was taking it to the neighborhood public oven. "May God be pleased with you," Zohra said as Meriem left. Zohra sat down again. "Isn't she sweet?" she said. Aziz nodded.

They finished breakfast. Zohra cleared the table and then announced that they had been invited to have lunch at her sister Samira's house, down in Zenata. She went to the bedroom to get her jellaba and slid it over her housedress. She stood facing him now. "If I go to Spain with you, who will take care of your mother?" she asked.

"My sisters," Aziz said, waving his hand. "She can go live with them. You've done more than enough." Aziz was the youngest in his family, and the responsibility for his mother would normally have gone to her daughters or to her firstborn, and he was neither.

Zohra nodded. Then she drew her breath and added, "But I don't speak Spanish."

"You'll learn. Just like I did."

"Couldn't you just stay here?"

Aziz shook his head. His lips felt dry and he wet them with his tongue. "We can talk about it later," he said.

THEY TOOK THE BUS to Samira's house. Aziz sat by a window and looked at the streets passing by. New buildings had sprung up everywhere, squat apartment houses with tiny windows that had been outlined with Mediterranean tile, in a futile attempt to render them more appealing. Internet cafés were now interspersed with tailor shops and hairdressers. He was startled away from the window when a bus coming in the other direction passed by, only inches away. Car horns blared from everywhere and motorcyclists barely slowed down at intersections.

They got off the bus and started walking. The smell of burned rubber made Aziz's nose feel stuffy. "Do you smell that?" he asked. Zohra shook her head. "It's a strong odor," he said. She shrugged. They passed a school and Aziz saw children playing a game of football on the grounds. It reminded him of his own childhood and he smiled. They arrived a little after the midday prayer. Samira answered the door, and Aziz was shocked to see her hair fully covered in one of those Islamic scarves that had seemed to multiply since he left. Collecting himself, he leaned over to give her a hug, but she stepped back from him and said, "Welcome, welcome."

Aziz straightened up. Unfazed, Zohra stepped in and took off her jellaba. They sat down on the foam-stuffed divan, and Mounir, Samira's husband, appeared. Aziz kept looking at Samira. Finally he asked, "When did you put on the hijab?"

"Two years ago," she said, "by the grace of God."

"Why?" Aziz asked.

"Because that is the right way," Zohra answered

Why was Zohra defending her? Aziz sat back. "So that means *you* are on the wrong path?" he asked her. Zohra shot him a look that said stop it. He pretended not to notice. "Well?"

Samira tilted her head. "May God put us all on the righteous path. Amen." She got up and started setting the table for lunch.

"How long will you be staying?" Mounir asked.

"Only ten days," Aziz said.

"He's going back again for a while," Zohra said.

Samira brought the plate of couscous. "You should go with him," she said. "Husbands and wives belong together."

Aziz watched for Zohra's reaction. Perhaps her own sister could convince her better than he could.

"I don't know if that's the life for me," Zohra said. But her tone was weak, and Aziz could see that her sister had planted a seed that he could cultivate until he convinced her.

THAT NIGHT ZOHRA came into the bedroom and turned off the light. But this time, when Aziz reached for her, she didn't turn away. He took her into his arms. It felt strange to be making love to her again. He had forgotten how small she was, and while he was on top of her he worried that his weight might be too much, so he supported himself on his forearms. Being with her brought to mind the women he had slept with while he was gone. He was ashamed to have cheated, but, he reasoned, he had been lonely and he was only human. He told himself that he had never intended to cheat on her, that the women he had slept with had meant nothing to him, just as, he was sure, he'd meant nothing to them. Now he wondered what his wife would look like in a sexy bustier, straddling him, her arms up in the air, moaning her pleasure out loud. He couldn't imagine Zohra doing it. But maybe she would, if he asked her. He came out of her and put his arm under her so he could scoop her up and put her on top of him, but she raised her head and gripped his arms in panic. Her eyes questioned him. He entered her again and resumed their lovemaking. When it was over and he lay in the dark, he wondered what had been on her mind. He feared that it was only one thing. He had seen how she had looked at the neighbor's child and he wondered if he should have stayed away from her tonight. He told himself that he'd have to use a condom next time. He didn't want to risk having children yet, not like this, not when they had to wait for her paperwork, not until he could support a family. He lay on the bed, unable to sleep.

A few days later Aziz went to visit his father's grave. Zohra led the way, walking swiftly among the rows of white headstones gleaming in the morning light. She stopped abruptly in front of one. Aziz's father's name, Abderrahman Ammor, was carved on it, followed by the prayer of the dead: *"O serene soul! Return to your Lord, joyful and pleasing in His sight. Join My followers and enter My paradise."* The date of his death followed: 27 Ramadan 1420.

Aziz recalled one day in 2000 when a letter had arrived announcing that his father had passed away. Zohra didn't have a telephone, so he had called the grocer and asked that someone get her. He had called back fifteen minutes later, but there was oddly little to say. By then his father has already been dead a month, and the event carried no urgency. He felt a great deal of shame at not being able to cry. In Madrid, life went on, and his grief, having no anchor, seemed never to materialize. Now he found it hard to conjure it on demand.

"I wish I had been there in his last days," Aziz said.

"The entire derb came to his wake," Zohra said.

Aziz got down on his knees and took out a brush from Zohra's bag. He started clearing the dead leaves from the headstone. "I wish I had been there," he said again.

Zohra kneeled next to him. "I don't want the same to happen to us. We should be together."

Aziz took a deep breath. He had waited for her to make up her mind, and now that she seemed to agree with him, he didn't feel the sense of joy he expected. When they left the cemetery, he told Zohra that he wanted to go for a walk before dinner, so while she took the bus home he headed downtown, to the Avenue des Forces Armées Royales. At the Café Saâda he peeked inside and saw the patrons standing at the bar or sitting in groups, huddled over their beers and gin tonics. On the terrace, customers sat indolently over their mint tea. He chose a seat outside, in the sun, and ordered an espresso. He looked around. Something struck him as odd, but he couldn't quite put a finger on it. It wasn't until the waiter came back with his coffee that he realized there were no women at all.

Some of the men played chess, others smoked, many read the newspaper. Those who sat closest to the stream of pedestrians passed the time by watching people, whistling every now and then if they saw a pretty girl. Aziz wondered why the place was so packed in the middle of the afternoon on a Wednesday, but the serious expression on everyone's face provided an answer to his question. They were unemployed. Aziz finished his coffee and left a generous tip before walking down the avenue. The fancy shops displayed leather goods, china, silk cushions, souvenirs, expensive wares that he knew most people in his neighborhood could never afford.

By the start of his second week in Casablanca, Aziz had seen every sibling, cousin, neighbor, and friend. He had heard about the weddings, births, and deaths. He had been appropriately shocked at how much his nieces and nephews had grown. But he found little else to do. The movie theaters showed films he'd already seen. He'd have liked to go to a nightclub, but he couldn't imagine Zohra going with him or even letting him go. Most of the programs on TV bored him, and unlike all their neighbors, Zohra refused to have a satellite dish. "No need to bring filth into the house, there's enough of it on the street" was how she put it. So he sat at home, on the divan, and waited for time to pass.

ON THE EVE of his departure, Aziz took his suitcase out of the armoire and began packing. Zohra sat on the bed, watching him. When he finished he took out a stack of bills from the inside pocket of his suitcase. He put the money in her hand. "This is all I have."

Zohra didn't move. She kept looking at him.

"I'll save more," he said, "and then I'll come back."

There was a skeptical look in Zohra's eyes, and it made Aziz feel uncomfortable. What did she expect of him? He couldn't give up an opportunity to work just so he could be at home with her. Did she have any idea what he'd gone through to make it in Spain? He couldn't give it all up now. He *had* to go back.

The grandfather clock chimed the hour.

"When are you sending me the papers?" she asked, at last.

"I don't know," he replied.

Zohra started crying. Aziz tapped her shoulder, in an awkward attempt at consolation. He couldn't imagine her with him in Madrid. She was used to the neighbor's kid pushing the door open and coming in. She was used to the outdoor market where she could haggle over everything. She was used to having her relatives drop in without notice. He couldn't think of her alone in an apartment, with no one to talk to, while he was at work. And he, too, had his own habits now. He closed his suitcase and lifted it off the bed. It felt lighter than when he had arrived.

The Storyteller

MURAD WAS SITTING behind the counter, reading a book, when the two women came in. It had been a quiet afternoon, disturbed only by the metronomic sound of the crackling radio at his feet, yet he'd had a hard time losing himself in the imagined world of the novel, even though it was set in Tangier. Or maybe it was because it was set in Tangier that he hadn't been able to reconcile the fictional world he was reading about with the one he experienced every day. He'd caught himself editing the author's prose—correcting an inaccurate reference and rewording the characters' dialogue—but that wasn't it. Something was missing. He'd gotten the book from the American Language Center, where neither of the overworked clerks bothered to check his long-expired membership card before stamping the book and handing it to him. He spent many hours there after work, trying to find something in the fiction section he hadn't yet read. There was another reason for his frequent visits to the center— a slender girl with lovely brown eyes who smiled at him over her copy of *Heart of Darkness* the first time he saw her. They'd just started seeing each other a couple of months ago. In time, Murad thought, he could introduce her to some of his favorite novels, the one in his hands at the moment not qualifying for that list.

The women's entry into Botbol Bazaar and Gifts provided a welcome distraction, and so he stood up, tossing the book aside. Anas, the other salesman, was slouched on a chair in the corner, snoring softly, as he did most afternoons. The owner was in Agadir on vacation, and Murad had been given the keys to the shop, much to the dismay of Anas, who'd been working there longer. Still, Murad got along reasonably well with him, mostly because he didn't mind when Anas took long breaks from the shop under the guise of going to get cigarettes or when he spent the afternoon asleep. Anas's head bobbed and jolted him awake. He looked around at the shop, saw the two women, and snapped to attention.

The women were both young, perhaps in their late twenties. One wore jeans and a loose henley shirt and a burlap bag whose strap crossed her chest, separating her breasts. Her strawberry blond hair was secured with a chopstick at the back of her head. Her friend, a dark-haired, heavy-set girl, was breathing heavily, having just come up the steep hillside street outside. Her blue shirt was stained under her arms, and she carried a handbag with the designer's name boldly proclaimed on the side. She walked straight to the jewelry case, where silver earrings were displayed next to coral-inlaid bracelets and amber bead necklaces. "How about something like this, Sandy?"

Sandy stood over the display case, looking bored and in a hurry to leave. "Jewelry is so personal," she said. "Your cousin might not like what you pick."

"Let's just take a look. How about that bracelet?"

"Oh, Chrissa," Sandy said, her shoulders dropping slightly. "I don't think it'd be appropriate for a wedding gift. Why don't you get her something for the house?"

Chrissa sighed dramatically, as though she'd been rushed by Sandy all afternoon and had had enough. "Fine," she said, walking from the jewelry case to the tables laden with souvenirs and knickknacks. Spotting a set of wooden tablets on a shelf, she squealed, "Look!"

Murad had purchased the tablets himself, on his boss's behalf, at an estate sale a few weeks before. They had been used in Quranic schools until the 1940s, but now, of course, it was increasingly rare to find any. The back of one tablet bore the name of the boy who'd used it (Taher) and the date (1935). It was unusual to have identifying details like this because the tablets were often returned when children finished school and reused by other students. On the front, the boy had written a verse from Sura 96, the very first verse to be revealed to the Prophet: "Read, in the name of thy Lord, who created." Murad had often wondered about the boy whose tablet had ended up at Botbol Bazaar and Gifts, whether he finished Quranic school and went on to public school or whether he'd been sent into an apprenticeship. He'd imagine Taher's life, making up parents and friends for him—a father who'd fought on the side of Abdelkrim in the Rif rebellion; a mother who desperately wanted a daughter; five older brothers; a sebsi-smoking neighbor who taught him the flute and the guenbri at night; a crush on a girl who lived up the street from him.

Chrissa picked up the tablet and held it up to the light to examine the writing. "The calligraphy looks beautiful," she said.

"I just love how the letters curve," Sandy said approvingly.

"It's an antique, I think."

Stuffing her hands in her jeans pocket, Sandy whispered, "Don't show too much interest, Chrissa, or they'll jack up the price." She affected a look of utter disinterest for the benefit of Anas, who sat in the corner watching them.

"Sorry," Chrissa said. She seemed like the kind of woman who always apologized for something. She carefully put the tablet down on the table, then grabbed at her long hair and peeled it from her neck, wiping the sweat with her hand. "It might work, don't you think," she whispered in a conspiratorial tone, "above the console in the entrance?"

Sandy nodded in approval. "I bet your cousin will like it."

But after staring at the tablet for a while, Chrissa moved on, Sandy shuffling behind her. "What's wrong? You don't like it anymore?" she asked.

"Sorry," Chrissa said. "I just want to see what else they've got."

"When we're done here, let's go check out Paul Bowles's house," Sandy said.

Murad wondered if it would ever be possible to get away from Bowles, from the dozens of tourists he seemed to inspire to come to Tangier, nostalgic for an era they never even knew. Was it his friendship with Kerouac and Ginsberg? The aura of mystery surrounding his marriage and his affairs? The myths he liked to create? Above all, Murad suspected, it was Bowles's stories that brought them, year after year. There had been a time in Murad's life when he'd used the author as bait, to lure tourists into guided tours of the city, but over time he'd grown weary of it.

He leaned with his elbows on the counter and opened his book again. He wanted to give the impression that he was lost in his reading, and he hoped that Anas, who was just now standing from the stool where he'd been perched, would take care of the two women so he wouldn't have to.

"I hope it's open to the public. Maybe we can take a picture there," Sandy said. Tapping her burlap bag, she added, "I brought the camera."

"I don't feel very photogenic today."

"Oh, stop it. You look fine."

"You know, I don't even think I've read anything by Bowles."

"Are you serious? Not even *The Sheltering Sky?*"

Chrissa shook her head. "Sorry."

"Wow. Then we really should go. It'll be fun, you'll see."

"So he lived here in Tangier?"

"Yep. Came here in the 1930s. It was Alice B. Toklas who advised him to go to Morocco," Sandy said. "And Gertrude Stein agreed, so he ended up here."

"Oh, really?" Chrissa said, absentmindedly. "Check this out." She pointed to a solid brass, horseshoe-shape mirror that hung from the wall, and seeing her reflection, she brushed her brown hair away from her face and pulled at her shirt.

Murad had a hard time keeping up the pretense, the lines blurring again before his eyes as he caught himself eavesdropping on the women. He hadn't indicated that he understood English, and even though Anas spoke Berber, Arabic, and Spanish, his English was limited to hello and good-bye. Eventually, Murad knew, if the women decided to buy something, he would have to disclose that he understood them, but for now he kept his eyes on his book even as he listened in.

"He lived here until his death."

"Who?"

"Bowles!" Sandy replied, her tone rising with her exasperation.

"Sorry," Chrissa said. "So he knew Morocco pretty well, then."

"Better than the Moroccans themselves."

WHEN HE WAS a little boy, Murad remembered, his father would sit down at night, cross-legged on the raffia mat, his back to the wall, and tell stories for him and for his sister Lamya. This was when the family still lived in the apartment downtown, before the birth of the twins and baby brother, before his father died and they had to move to the one-bedroom in the medina. He remembered the stories only in fragments, names like Juha and Aisha rising to his consciousness now, pieces of a puzzle that he couldn't reconstruct. Realizing this, he felt at once angry and sad, as though he had just discovered that a part of him was missing. He stared at the page for a long time, trying to bring back the memory of a single story.

Childhood images of ogres and jinns flickered in his mind's eye, but he could not hang on to any of them. His father started every story with "Kan, ya ma kan," "Once there was and there was not." The timeless opening line was fitting, it seemed to him, to the state he found himself in now, unable to ascertain whether the tales he remembered were real or figments of his imagination. The deep baritone of his father's voice echoed in his ears, strong and reassuring, and finally one story slowly unraveled for him, the tale of Aisha Qandisha. For days after his father had told the story, Murad had had nightmares that the goat-footed ogress was running after him, calling out his name in a sweet voice, and he was tempted to turn around and look at her, but he couldn't because he knew she would cast a spell on him.

"What do you think about this?" Chrissa asked. She pointed to a Berber rug hanging from the ceiling.

"It's beautiful," Sandy said. "Nice workmanship, too."

"I just love the animal patterns," Chrissa said. "It would be perfect as a wedding gift, wouldn't it?"

"Careful, you're being too eager," Sandy said.

"Hello," Anas said.

"See," Sandy said. She smiled at Anas, but with a distance that suggested she was not interested so please don't even start. Anas smiled blithely, the extent of his English having been exhausted. He wore a football shirt and washed-out jeans, and he shuffled in his yellow belgha to the light switch, which he turned on, illuminating the display cases. He gestured with his hand that the women were welcome to explore the merchandise upstairs, but they remained where they were, undecided about the rug.

When he'd returned to Tangier a year before, Murad had gone home and refused to go out. He avoided family gatherings, refused to run errands, turned down offers to play soccer with the neighbors. Everyone knew he'd tried to go to Spain, and now they all knew he'd been caught and deported, so he took to staying home with his mother, forsaking even a glass of tea at the Café La Liberté with the other unemployed young men from the neighborhood. He watched his mother as she worked around the house, cleaning or cooking, her bracelets clinking with every movement of her wrists. He'd waited for a reasonable amount of time to pass before he'd asked her for them, asked her to sell them and lend him the money so he could try to go to Spain again. "Have you lost your mind?" she'd said. "Haven't you learned your lesson? I would never do it, so don't ask me again." But Murad asked her again and again, and each time she ignored him. "Can you pass the bread?" she'd say, or, "It looks like it's going to rain." She acted as though she was doing him a favor by glossing over an indiscreet remark on his part. It was infuriating, being ignored like this. By then he was spending a lot of time alone with her at home, his sister having married and moved out, the twins still away in college, and his younger brother in school most of the day. They were like an old couple, having breakfast together, watching TV together, increasingly accustomed to the sounds they made throughout the day—the gurgling of the water she used for her ablutions, the creaking of the cabinet door he opened to get his shirts. When his brother-in-law, Lamya's husband, told him that one of his clients, an old man whose children had immigrated to Israel, needed help at his shop, Murad had jumped on the offer.

Even after he took the job, Murad couldn't help but wonder what lay ahead. If he hadn't set foot in Spain, it would have been easier to dismiss his fantasies of what could have been; but he had made it to Tarifa, so every day he daydreamed about the life he thought he would have had. Now, he realized, he'd had it wrong. He'd been so consumed with his imagined future that he hadn't noticed how it had started to overtake something inside him, bit by bit. He'd been living in the future, thinking of all his tomorrows in a better place, never realizing that his past was drifting. And now, when he thought of the future, he saw himself in front of his children, as mute as if his tongue had been cut off, unable to recount for them the stories he'd heard as a child. He wondered if one always had to sacrifice the past for the future, or if it was something he had done, something peculiar to him, an inability to fill himself with too much, so that for every new bit of imagined future, he had to forsake a tangible past.

"It's gorgeous," Chrissa whispered.

"Muy lindo," Anas said.

Chrissa smiled politely, looking up at the geometric motif. Sandy sighed. "Well, now that he's here, you might as well ask him what part of Morocco the rug is from."

Chrissa turned to Anas and in accented Spanish asked him Sandy's question. She waited to hear the answer and then translated for Sandy. "From Nader? Nador? Someplace like that."

"Ah. Traditional Berber rugs are usually warm-colored like this one. And look at the animal motifs. Brings to mind some of those Native American drawings, doesn't it?"

Chrissa nodded in agreement.

The carpet came from a small workshop that had been doing business with Botbol Bazaar for more than twenty years. The owner had died only two months ago, and it was his son who'd brought the latest shipment, carrying each rug into the shop himself. The memory triggered another one, and so Murad remembered another story his father had told, about a young rug weaver and the revenge he took on the man who'd stolen his beloved.

"¿Quieren un te?" Anas asked.

"Oh, I don't know if it's necessary," Chrissa said. "He's asking if we want tea."

"I understood that," Sandy said. "Trust me, they *want* you to have tea."

Chrissa seemed to doubt her friend, but deferred to her anyway.

"Si," Sandy said to Anas, forcefully nodding her head.

Anas smiled and signaled to Murad that he was going to get the tea.

"You're probably going to get suckered into buying something anyway," Sandy said, "so we might as well have a cup of tea while we're here." She sat down on a chair in the corner and looked around her. "Maybe later we can stop by one of the cafés where Bowles used to hang out," she said brightly. Suddenly noticing an old leather trunk to her right, she bent over it, admiring the patterns made by the nails. With her finger, she wrote something in the layer of dust.

Chrissa, who'd been sitting quietly with her purse on her lap, turned to look at Murad and, knowing he had seen this, gave him an apologetic look. Murad smiled at her and came out from behind the counter. He wheeled a round tea table over and set it on its legs in front of the girls. "Welcome, welcome," he said.

If she was surprised, Sandy didn't let on, as though she had expected him to speak English all along.

"Really, there's no need for tea," Chrissa said.

"Please," he said, "it's a pleasure." He sat down, crossed his legs. "So you're interested in Paul Bowles?" he asked.

"Sure," said Sandy, her face lighting up. "Have you read him?"

Murad nodded.

"I love his books," she said, waving a fly away from her face. Her green eyes were lined with kohl. "He's such a wonderful storyteller."

"Shall I tell you a story, then, while we wait for tea?" Murad asked.

Sandy's eyes sparkled with interest, and glancing delightedly at Chrissa, she said, "Sure!"

"Once there was, and there was not, a rug weaver named Ghomari. He was known and admired throughout the land for the tapestries he weaved, and people came from far and wide to buy his work. Ghomari was in love with a beautiful young woman, who was promised to him. She was the daughter of the muezzin and her name was Jenara. From time to time, Jenara would come watch Ghomari work, and she would ask him how long it would take before he would save enough money for her dowry. 'I have to sell ten more carpets,' he'd say, or, 'Only seven more, my love,' and invariably she would say, 'Hurry up and sell them, then, so we can get married.'

"One day Jenara had come to watch Ghomari work in

his shop in the middle of the afternoon. It was unbearably hot, and so young Jenara sat with her back to the street and unveiled her face. At that moment, the midget Arbo, who was as ugly as he was evil, happened by, and when he saw that Ghomari was busy talking to someone whom he couldn't see, he jumped inside the shop and saw Jenara unveiled. He was struck dumb by her beauty, and he was still speechless when Ghomari, cursing him, threw him out of the shop.

"From then on, Arbo harassed young Jenara, wherever she was, whether she was on her way to the market or going to the hammam, making declarations of love. Jenara yelled at him. 'I would rather be dead than become your wife.' Arbo walked away, already fomenting ways in which he could get revenge. He went to his master, the Sultan, and told him he'd seen the most beautiful woman in the entire kingdom, but she was promised to a simple rug weaver. Hearing this, the Sultan said, 'How can a rug weaver have a more beautiful wife than I? Do what you must.' And so Arbo waited for the muezzin to be up on the minaret making the call to kidnap Jenara and take her into the Sultan's harem. The poor girl spent her days crying over her forced marriage to the brutal Sultan, and none of the gifts the Sultan bestowed on her could quiet her crying.

"Poor Ghomari knew that there was no use fighting the Sultan who'd stolen his beloved, so he turned to his tapestry and poured his sorrow into it. He weaved a rug that showed Jenara in all her beauty, her face unveiled, and in her hand a long knife, representing his desire for revenge. When he was done, he marveled at his own creation, which was so lifelike that it was as though Jenara was standing right before him, ready to strike. Ghomari gathered his father and Jenara's father and showed them the tapestry. They, too, were amazed by the rug, and so they told their wives, who told their sisters, who told their husbands.

"And so, every night, after dark, Ghomari would close his shop to hold viewing sessions of this most marvelous tapestry, until Arbo got word of it. He told the Sultan about the tapestry, and soon enough it was confiscated and Ghomari was put in jail. When the Sultan cast his eyes on it, he was taken once again with how beautiful Jenara looked, but, even more, by the terrifying expression on her face. He showed it to his court, delighting in their reactions, and had it hung in his bedroom. When he next saw Jenara, he told her that Ghomari was to be executed by morning. Jenara didn't show any sadness over the death of her betrothed. The Sultan asked his trusted

Arbo why that might be. The midget replied that perhaps Jenara had finally seen the light. Over the next few weeks, Jenara seemed happy, chatting and joking with Arbo. 'This is how women are,' Arbo told his master. 'Sometimes they have to be shown a strong hand before they'll learn what's good for them.'

"One night, Jenara told Arbo that she had long desired a beautiful bracelet, but that its owner, a jeweler in the Mellah, didn't want to part with it. Arbo said, 'Fear not, mistress, I will get it for you this very night.' And so Arbo took off for the Mellah, leaving his post beside his master. Jenara walked into the Sultan's bedroom, a knife in her hand."

Anas arrived with the teapot and four stacked glasses, which he put on the table and started serving. "Very sweet," Chrissa said, tasting her tea. "Delicious."

"How does your story end?" Sandy asked.

"Jenara held the knife to the Sultan's throat, who woke up in terror. He called out to his faithful Arbo, but the midget had gone to fetch the imaginary bracelet. The Sultan cried and writhed in fear. Members of his court came rushing in, and Jenara retreated against the rug hanging on the wall. 'She's trying to kill me!' he screamed, pointing at the young girl. 'But Master, that is only your tapestry on the wall.' The Sultan cried out to them that they were to seize her, but none of his retinue moved.

" 'He's lost his mind,' said the Grand Vizir, and he left to go share the news with the Sultan's younger brother, whom the Sultan had locked away in a dark gaol. The Vizir was eager to curry favor with the man who would soon replace the demented on the throne. Members of the court disappeared one by one, shaking their head over their master who'd gone mad. After the door had closed, Jenara finally brought the knife to the Sultan's throat and killed him.

"She and Ghomari had finally gotten their revenge."

"Wow," Sandy said. "That's brutal."

Chrissa turned around to look at the carpet behind her. Anas refilled the glasses and asked, "¿Le gusta la alfombra?"

"Si," Chrissa said.

Sandy laughed. "Really, Chrissa, is that all it takes?"

"Well, I think it would look beautiful in my cousin's living room," Chrissa replied, pursing her lips. "And I'm going to buy it."

"Fine," Sandy said. "Let's just get it and leave. I want to get to Bowles's house before it closes." She looked at her watch.

"How much?" Chrissa asked.

"Mil quiniento," Anas said.

"He wants fifteen hundred for it," Chrissa translated.

Murad thought Anas must have liked the girl a lot, because he started the bargaining at such a low price. That carpet was worth twelve hundred, much more if it was sold in a fancy shop downtown.

"Too much," Sandy said, leaning forward in her chair, eager to bargain, the way her guidebooks probably told her she should. "Six hundred."

Murad raised an eyebrow.

"Are you sure?" Chrissa asked her friend, turning to look at her. Sandy nodded.

The radio crackled with the sound of the four o'clock news. Murad turned his tea glass in his hand several times. "My friend made a mistake," he said at last. "The price is eighteen hundred."

Sandy blinked. "One thousand," she said.

"Twelve hundred," Murad said, standing. "My last price."

"Fine," Chrissa said, opening her purse.

"You'll probably get three times that much for it on eBay," Sandy said, shrugging.

Murad went back to sit behind the counter, leaving Anas to run the credit card and wrap the rug for them. He picked up his book, smoothed the edge of the page he'd marked by folding a corner, and closed it for good. There was no use reading stories like this anymore; he needed to write his own. He thought about his father, who'd told stories to his children, and how they were almost forgotten today. Anas closed the cash register with a loud ring, but Murad hardly paid any attention; he was already lost in the story he would start writing tonight.

ACKNOWLEDGMENTS

FOR THEIR COMMENTS on portions of this manuscript, in various guises, I thank Mary Akers, Judith Beck, Katrina Denza, Alicia Gifford, Carrie Hernández, Kirsten Menger-Anderson, and Rob Roberge.

I am also indebted to Randa Jarrar, Maud Newton, and Mark Sarvas, for their faith and encouragement; Junot Díaz, Whitney Otto, and Diana Abu-Jaber, for their generosity; Lana Salah Barkawi, Lee Chapman, Susan Muaddi Darraj, and Tracey Cooper, for wonderful boosts during the writing of this book; and Shabnam Fani, for the gift of time.

Many thanks to my agent, Stéphanie Abou, for her patience and dedication; my friends at the Joy Harris Literary Agency, for their commitment; my editor, Antonia Fusco, for her judicious comments and enthusiasm; and everyone at Algonquin Books, for their hard work.

Thank you to my parents, Ahmed and Madida Lalami, for many spirited discussions during the writing of this book; my sister and my brothers, who always acted as though I could, and so I did; and Sophie, for never letting me forget what matters most.

Above all, thanks to Alexander Yera, for keeping the faith, even when I didn't.